Reclaimed Assurance

GAYLENE NUNN

WEEZIE PUBLISHING

ISBN: 9798985879902

gaylenenunn.com

Contents

I dedicate this book to all my family and friends who have encouraged me through the process of writing this book.

"We're never so vulnerable than when we trust some-one - but paradoxically, if we cannot trust, neither can we find love or joy."—Walter Anderson

Madison swings around and glares at Brody, shaking his hand away. "Mr. McGuire, how dare you to assume I'm that type of woman." She quickly turns and almost runs to the exit.

"Madison, wait," Brody says, trying to catch up to her. Madison pretends not to hear and keeps walking quickly. As she gets to her car and opens her door, the warm, muscular hand is placed on top of hers.

A tingling sensation runs up her arm, momentarily confusing her, and she jerks her hand away.

"Madison, please wait and let me explain," Brody says, sounding earnest.

"Then, start explaining because I don't have all night," she demands.

Brody backs up, giving Madison space. "I was supposed to meet a woman here tonight at 7:00. I met her on a dating app. She goes by the name Looking for a Friend. Since my date and yours didn't show, I wondered if you might be her."

"Oh, my gosh! Are you Lonesome Guy from Knoxville?"

Brody grins from ear to ear. "I am, so can we start tonight over?" Madison smiles. "Hi! I'm Brody McGuire, AKA Lonesome Guy from Knoxville." He reaches his hand out to her.

"Hello, Brody. I'm Madison Donaldson, AKA Searching for a Friend. It's nice to meet you," she shakes his hand.

"Shall we have dinner now?" Madison nods. Brody offers his arm to her, and they walk back into the restaurant together. The tingling sensation happens again, confusing Madison even more.

Chapter 1

MADISON

Pineville, Kentucky, is what some people consider one of the best small towns to live in. It is between Pine Mountain and the Cumberland River. Pineville is approximately three hours from Knoxville, Tennessee, and Lexington, Kentucky. The area features many outdoor activities, including fishing and tourism. So it only made sense to come back to Pineville when I retired, Madison Donaldson thinks as she sits on the deck of her cabin.

Only the COVID pandemic made it possible to move earlier than she had planned. She could work remotely, so Madison sold her townhouse in Nashville and moved back to Pineville. The town she left forty years ago. Working remotely proved to be a challenge. The cabin's Wi-Fi was problematic, forcing Madison to rent a small office from Bruce Benson, her financial advisor, and childhood friend.

"My cabin," Madison yells at the top of her lungs. "Mine. All mine now." She takes a sip from the red wine she poured to celebrate the day. Although Madison has been living in the cabin for two years, today was the day she sent the money to her brother in Seattle to buy his share of the place. The five acres of land, one-acre pond, and cabin their parents left to them is now hers.

Madison reaches for her notepad and pen lying next to her wineglass. She looks over her to-do list. A few items were crossed off, like the state-of-the-art security system and kitchen upgrades, but more must be done. Madison adds a security gate at the entrance to the property and stocking the one-acre pond with fish to her list.

Her cell phone ringing disrupts her thoughts, and Madison picks up the phone happy to discover it is Bruce calling. "Bruce, hi. We haven't talked in a long time."

"Hilarious, Madison. We just saw each other five hours ago."

"I know, but you gave me so much to think about. It seems like years."

Bruce laughs at the comment. "Yes, it's a lot to think about. Congratulations on finally owning the property. I'm glad your jerk brother finally agreed to sell."

"Well, he always was a jerk, but you know that as well as I do."

"I thought of one more thing for you to consider about moving into town. With your Wi-Fi being so spotty, it could affect your consulting work. I just wanted to remind you of that."

"I hadn't thought of that, so thanks for bringing it up."

"Okay, that's all I have to say. Oh, one more thing. Perry wants to know if you'll have dinner with us next week?"

"Well, tell Perry yes, but only if he cooks one of his gourmet dinners," Madison answers.

"Gourmet dinners? Aren't you tired of his spaghetti and meatballs? I know I am."

"Well, yes, but I didn't want to hurt his feelings," Madison laughs.

"Great. I'll get takeout. I'll let you know what day. Love you, Mads!"

"Love you bunches, Bru," Madison says, hanging up the phone and placing it on the table. She looks at the empty wineglass and goes to the kitchen to refill it. When she sits back down, she stares at the pond as if expecting a fish to jump out of the water and give her the answers she needs.

Bruce informed Madison this morning that she has until the year-end to purchase some property. If she doesn't reinvest the money, she will have to pay taxes on the money she got from selling the townhouse. He suggested she buy a house in town for safety reasons and now Wi-Fi for her consulting business.

Although never concerned about her safety at the cabin, Madison realized she didn't have any neighbors to call on in the event of an emergency. Like last year, she broke her right leg and had to drive herself to the hospital with her left leg. Dang, I almost ran over the mountainside twice on the drive. Madison remembers and shivers.

Bruce suggested renting the cabin as a vacation home to tourists this morning. With a well-stocked pond, people could fish as well as swim. Then, all Madison would have to do was create a website for the rentals, clean the cabin, and ensure it was stocked with linens for guests. "But this was my family's vacation house, and it has so many memories," she told Bruce. He said he understood because he spent much time there with her family. "I don't need the additional income either," Madison said. Bruce agreed with that, but he reminded her she was getting older. Plus, she would be closer to Bruce and Perry if she needed help.

"Bruce gave me a lot to think about," Madison says aloud. Maybe I'll look around town and see what houses are available. That should keep Bruce happy for a little while. He has a point because I need reliable Wi-Fi for my business. I hate using his office space because he needs to hire someone to help him since his business is really growing.

Madison sits on the deck for a few more minutes and finishes her wine. Then she goes inside and makes a sandwich, bringing it back to the deck so she can eat and watch the sun go down on the warm Spring day. She thinks I'll miss this view and the peace if I move to town.

Chapter 2

MADISON

Four months later, Madison sits on her sofa in her new three-bedroom, two-bath house in Pineville. The house is in a gated, over 55+ community, three blocks from Bruce and Perry. Although she never has house guests, one bedroom is furnished. However, Bruce and Perry have guests, and their extra guests can always stay at her house. Madison turned the third bedroom into an office.

Things are looking suitable for the cabin rental, Madison thinks to herself. Perry helped her create a website, and her first guests will arrive tomorrow. She also landed two consulting jobs and is bidding on one more. But it is her personal life that's lacking, Madison determines. Any friends she had in school, other than Bruce, are tied up with their kids and grandkids. But, of course, there are new people in Pineville now, and Madison has met a few at various functions. Some are only interested in their country club activities, and others prefer to hang out at local bars—none of those options interest Madison.

This morning, Madison spent two hours on the phone with Beverly, a friend Madison met several years ago at a Human Resources conference. Beverly, like Madison, doesn't have many friends and lives in a small town in Arizona. Beverly mentioned a new singles website for professionals she found. She told Madison this new site was different. Members do not post pictures or ages. Instead, members are matched based on their interests, career, current employment, and other basic information.

For most of her life, Madison shied away from men after a disastrous marriage forty years ago. It took her fifteen years to go out with a man. After that, Madison had a few affairs but nothing long-term which suited her. Truth be told, she didn't trust men.

Still, the website sounded interesting. Madison had been on a few before but found the men usually only looked at the pictures. The women that always got the most interest wore low-cut tops showing off their boobs. Many people had told Madison she was beautiful, but she never believed them. Now the tiny wrinkles were showing around her eyes. Also, the scars on her body led to more insecurities.

Grabbing her laptop, Madison checks out the website. After carefully reading the Terms and Conditions, she creates an account using the name "Searching for a Friend". Madison chooses not to go into much detail about her career, only stating that it was in Human Resources and that she worked in the banking field. She adds she is retired and doing consulting work. In the Education section, Madison entered her undergraduate and graduate degrees from the University of Louisville, but not the years.

Madison struggles with the Hobbies/Interests section. She finally decides on following some of the University of Louisville sports, fundraising for the local humane society, reading, and traveling. But, the most challenging section is what she is looking for in a man. I'll be honest and see what happens, Madison decides. She types in that she wants a friend foremost. A man she can talk to and enjoy being with. Perhaps, someone that wishes to travel and share experiences and sights. Madison adds that the man should be happy in his own skin and enjoy quiet time. "There," she says aloud. "Now let's see what happens."

Chapter 3

BRODY

"Just do it, Brody," Angela says, rolling her eyes.

"No, it's stupid."

"Brody, what's stupid is your company just bought one of the most successful dating apps in the US, and you're not using it."

"Angela, I would fire you now if you hadn't already worked for me for twenty years. I said drop it," Brody says, unable to hide his smile.

"Haha. You would be so lost without me. You're a wealthy, handsome businessman who would be a great catch." Brody rolls his eyes at her remark. "Just try it. I'll even help you write the profile for it."

"Good gosh, no! You will not write a profile for me. Besides, I need no more female vampires chasing after me for my money. I need a friend is what I need. You and Ted are about the only real friends I have."

Angela stares at Brody for a few moments. He's always referred to her as a mother hen, even though she's ten years younger than him, but never a friend. "A minute ago, you wanted to fire me, and now I'm your friend. So make up your feeble mind, Brody."

Brody sighs. "You know what I mean. I'm lonesome and just want someone to talk to and spend time with without obligations or commitments. Can you understand that?"

"Yeah, I really do, Brody. You also need to get away for a few days and relax."

"Where would I go, Angela? Everyone knows who I am and what I do, so I doubt I'll have any peace."

"Brody, let me search the internet and find you a place. Now I have work to do, and you need to think about doing a profile on that dating site. Have you ever looked at the site?"

"No, I haven't had a reason to. Why?"

"It's different. There are no pictures or names. Instead, interests, education, careers, and basic information are used to select matches. Just look at it." Angela leaves the office, closing the door behind her softly.

Brody watches her leave and turns to look out the windows of his highrise office building. Maybe I should look at the site. If pictures aren't used, no one would recognize me, and he thinks I could be as vague as I want on the profile. Sitting down at his desk, Brody opens the app and reads over the terms and conditions.

"What the heck," Brody says aloud. He selects a profile name and types in very basic information into his profile, not wanting to give too much away. I am tired of women looking for a rich husband, and so many women I know are so shallow. I'm too old for games. "That's enough," Brody says aloud when he's finished the profile. "Now, let's see what happens."

Chapter 4

BRODY

Monday morning the following week, Angela enters Brody's office without knocking. "I've found the perfect getaway spot for you."

"Don't you knock anymore?"

"Why should I? I can see you weren't on the phone, and I knew no one was here."

"I'm still considering firing you," Brody replies with a smile.

"Do it. I would love to stay home with three kids all day." Angela declares.

Brody laughs, knowing she is lying. "So, tell me about this ideal spot you found for me."

Angela walks around his desk and elbows him to move over so she can reach his keyboard. She types in the website address, and a cabin surrounded by woods appears on the monitor. "Okay, look at this. It is isolated, surrounded by woods." She clicks on the following picture. "It has a one-acre pond stocked with fish, and they furnish the fishing equipment. Like you have any. It is five miles from the nearest town and only three hours away."

"That looks interesting. I haven't fished in years and years. So what's the catch?"

"There's no catch to it. Furnish your food and leave the cabin clean. They leave the key in a convenient location, and you see no one unless you go into town. There's a gate at the entrance to keep people out."

"Hmmm," Brody says as he takes the mouse away from Angela and clicks on the website's pictures. "Call and see when the first available weekend is and book me for Friday, Saturday, and Sunday nights."

"I'll do that." Angela clamps her hand down on Brody's shoulder and squeezes. "I'm excited now if you would only get on that dating website."

"I already did. I made a profile, but there have been no matches yet," Brody says, turning his chair around to face her.

"OMG!" Angela exclaims. "I can't believe it."

"Well, I'll do just about anything to get you off my back."

Angela laughs as she turns and heads to the door. "Baby steps, Brody. Baby steps."

The next couple of days are so busy for Brody that he never gives the dating app another thought. That is, until late Wednesday, when a message pops up on his laptop. Curious, he opens the app and finds it has found him a match. Brody reads the woman's profile several times and is pleased to discover she is searching for friendship, not a relationship. Plus, she sounds interesting. *I'll wait until tomorrow to send her a message,* Brody decides. *That will give him time to contemplate what he wants to say.*

Chapter 5

MADISON

Madison spends the first of the following week working on her bid proposal. The guests at the cabin left fantastic reviews on several websites, and the cabin is booked for the next month. But, so far, no one has shown an interest in her profile, which doesn't surprise her. Unfortunately, Madison's pleasant week hits a snag on Thursday. She must travel for one of her consulting jobs, leaving no one to tend to the cabin.

"Bruce," Madison yells, walking into his reception area. Fortunately, the room is empty except for Bruce's assistant. "I have an enormous problem!"

"Madison, you don't have to yell," Bruce says, opening his office door. "I'm not hard of hearing yet."

"Bruce, I have to leave for Denver on Sunday, and I don't have anyone to help with the cabin."

"Madison, calm down. Perry and I can help until you find someone."

"Excuse me," Bridgette, Bruce's assistant, says. "I can help. I could use the extra money for school clothes for the kids."

15

"Bridgette, it would require some weekend work. Would you be okay with that?" Madison asks.

"Heck yeah, if it's quiet at the cabin. It would be good to be away from the kids for a while. Howard can deal with them," Bridgette says with a smirk.

Bruce laughs. "Howard with four kids? That should be interesting."

"I know, right?" Bridgette says with a big smile. Madison looks from one to the other, confused. "Madison, Howard doesn't keep the kids very often. I look forward to hearing about this."

"Great, and thanks, Bridgette. Let's try it out over the weekend. Can you meet me at the cabin after work to review everything? I have guests coming in tomorrow afternoon," Madison states.

"Sure thing, if we can do it about 6:00. That will give me time to pick up burgers for Howard and the kids for dinner."

"Perfect, and I'll leave the gate open for you. Thanks again, Bridgette. You're a lifesaver."

"Madison," Bruce says, "please don't yell next time. I might have a client."

"Well, you are getting up in years," Madison replies with a quick peck on Bruce's cheek. Then she turns and walks out the door with a wave.

Bridgette arrives at the cabin promptly at 6:00. She carefully takes notes as Madison goes over all the details of what should be done and when. She shows Bridgette the list of rules guests have to follow and what to do if the rules aren't followed. Madison assures Bridgette that she will take care of any reservations while traveling.

Breathing a sigh of relief, Madison returns home and sits down with a glass of wine, tossing her cell phone on the couch next to her. About halfway through the wine, Madison's cell phone pings with an unfamiliar sound. She picks it up to find a message on the singles app. Shocked, Madison reaches for her laptop, clicks on the message icon, and opens the website.

"Hi, Searching for a Friend. I am a Lonesome Guy in Knoxville. I, too, am looking for a friend. A real friend that doesn't judge me and is interested in me as a person."

Madison reads the message several times, trying to decide how to respond. Then she types, *"Hi, Lonesome Guy in Knoxville. I don't judge people, but go with my gut instincts."*

"I like that response. Please read my profile and let me know what you think. Good night."

Okay, Madison thinks. She goes to Lonesome Guy in Knoxville's profile and reads it slowly. It says he is looking for a friend to spend time with on the weekends because he owns his own business and is very busy during the week. His career is in technology. Lonesome Guy has a degree in Computer Science from the University of Kentucky (UK). He likes most sports and, of course, follows UK's teams. Lonesome Guy states he's laid back but has to attend formal functions, which he finds extremely dull. Madison laughs aloud because she totally gets that statement. Lonesome Guy says he likes to travel, but most of his travel is business related. That's it. That's all his profile says, which doesn't tell me much about him, Madison decides. I'll sleep on it and respond to him tomorrow.

Chapter 6

BRODY

Brody wakes Thursday morning excited at the prospect of a message from his dating app match. Although busy with meetings all day, he checks the app several times, hoping for a message, but each time, he's disappointed.

After a long day, Brody arrives home at 6:30. His housekeeper has dinner waiting for him as usual. He sits down to eat, and his phone pings with a notice. Brody starts not to check it, fearing it is about work. But, he decides he should because there are several vital contracts in the works. He is pleasantly surprised to see the message from his match, Searching for a Friend.

Her message is a straightforward statement in response to his. Brody wants to keep it simple, so he asks her to read his profile and tell him what she thinks. Then, he signs off good night. Brody reads her profile several times before going to bed.

Searching for a Friend is educated and retired but doing consulting work. That's interesting, Brody thinks. She worked in the Human Resources field, which meant she had to keep up with changes in laws and the work environment and deal with many people and problems.

Searching for a Friend graduated from the University of Louisville, Brody's alma mater's biggest rival. That would lead to interesting conversations, he determines.

Her profile also states that she does fundraising for the local animal shelter society and likes to read and travel. What catches Brody's eye most is what she is searching for in a man. The profile says Searching for a Friend is seeking a friend she can have conversations with while enjoying being together. Perhaps, someone that wants to travel and share experiences. She wants a man that is comfortable in his own skin and enjoys quiet time.

That night, Brody lies in bed thinking about the profile. This woman has piqued his interest. But, just by the few things he's read, Brody senses, Searching for a Friend is not the typical woman he usually meets or goes out with. He snorts. Goes out with? That's funny. For many years, going out with a woman meant going to some formal function, followed by sex at her house and then home. Recently, Brody stopped doing that, preferring to go to functions alone, and his sex life has become nonexistent. Phony women with phony body parts or parts pumped up with Botox did nothing for him anymore. Even the new women in town, his best friend, Ted, introduced him to, didn't phase him.

Brody looks at the clock beside his bed, surprised to see it is 2:00 am. I better get some sleep, but first, I'll send a quick message to Searching for a Friend.

Chapter 7

MADISON

"*D*id *you read my profile?*" the waiting message says when Madison opens the website the next morning.

"*I did, and I feel the same way about formal functions,*" Madison types. "*So many people use the events as an excuse to get drunk and act stupid. I enjoy dressing up occasionally, though. As far as you being a UK fan, that may be a deal breaker.*" Madison hits the send button and smiles. "Well, let's see if he has a humorous side."

As she sets the laptop down, a message pops up. "*I could say the same thing about a U of L fan, but I try not to judge people with poor taste too harshly. And, yes, formal events seem to bring out the worst in people.*"

It appears he has a sense of humor, Madison thinks. "*Poor taste? I'll have you know I paid a great deal of money to have that poor taste,*" she writes and sends.

"*I'm not sure about you, though. A University of Louisville fan is strike one in my book. Banking, as a career, is strike two,*" Lonesome Guy sends.

20

Madison stares at the screen for a few seconds, trying to determine what to write. Hmmm. It's a baseball analogy. *"Okay, Lonesome Guy. That's two strikes. It is at the bottom of the ninth. The game's tied, and the bases are loaded. What's your pitch?"* Madison answers.

Lonesome Guy's reply comes in a few seconds. *"Interesting question, because you might strike out if I throw a fastball. Then the game would be over."*

"True, but there's always a chance to get a hit on a fastball. Or the fastball could be high and away. Or it could be low and inside. Either way, that could mean a walk and a run scores."

"Hmmm. I believe I'll save that last pitch because I'm not ready to end the game."

"Me either," Madison answers. She waits, but no more messages appear. At least he didn't ask for my email address to communicate with me as many scammers do, Madison thinks. Now, I need to get to work. She puts the laptop away, eats a quick breakfast, and heads to the cabin.

She checks the cabin to make sure it is ready for her latest guests. Then Madison places fresh linens in the storage closet for Bridgette's use. The weekend guests are scheduled to leave Monday morning, but another group is booked to arrive on Tuesday, staying through the weekend. Madison will be back on Wednesday and will take over from Bridgette then. After she leaves the cabin, Madison stops at the hardware store and has spare keys made for Bridgette, which she drops off at Bruce's office. Finally, Madison picks up her suits at the cleaners and heads home to pack for her trip.

After a quick dinner, Madison selects two suits for her trip. Next, she texts a friend in Denver to see if she can meet for dinner one night. While waiting for her friend to respond, a message pops up from Lonesome Guy.

"Hi.
I hope you had a good day. I have a question for you."

"So now the twenty questions begin," Madison responds.

"No, just one question, I promise. Why are you just looking for a friend?"

How do I answer, Madison asks herself? I'll answer honestly because I have nothing to lose. *"I have trust issues with men."*

"Thank you for being honest. I have trust issues with women."

Madison decides not to reply because she doesn't know what to say, and she closes the website showing she is offline. Her friend says she can meet for dinner any night, so they decide on Monday night at a popular Denver restaurant. Madison waits until the next day to pack and heads to bed.

Chapter 8

BRODY

"**B**rody! Brody!"

"Why are you yelling at me, and what do you want, Angela?"

"What is wrong with you?"

"I got very little sleep last night. I'll ask again what do you want?" Brody asks, looking at Angela standing in his doorway.

"I'm just reminding you there's a meeting in an hour in the conference room to discuss possible changes to the dating app. Now that you're on it, maybe you'll understand and be able to take part in the discussion," Angela says with a smirk.

"I'm not an idiot. I doubt I would have bought the company if I hadn't understood before now. Promise me you won't say a word about me being on the app?" Brody says with tired, pleading eyes.

"Don't worry, because I value my life too much. Besides, in my will, I left the kids to you, which I'm sure you'd enjoy," Angela replies with a wave and closes the door.

Brody places his elbows on his desk and his head in his hands. I hope this meeting goes by fast. I have time for a nap before my next appointment if it does. Ping, his phone goes off with a message. It's from Searching for a Friend.

She read his profile, and that's a good sign. She said she shares his feelings about social events and appears to have a sense of humor, teasing him about being a UK fan.

Brody messages her back immediately, teasing her about being a University of Louisville fan and having poor taste.

Searching for a Friend responds she paid a lot of money to have her poor taste, which makes Brody laugh aloud.

Wanting to tease her more and see if she was honest about liking sports, Brody uses baseball terms in his following message. He tells Searching for a Friend that being a U of L fan is one strike against her and working in banking is a second strike.

Searching for a Friend's response catches Brody off guard. She wrote, "*okay, Lonesome Guy. That's two strikes, and it is the bottom of the ninth. The game's tied, and bases are loaded. What's your pitch?*"

Oh my gosh, Brody thinks. I like this woman already. He continues the back-and-forth exchange by saying if I throw a fastball, you could strike out, and it's over.

Searching for a Friend responds by agreeing, but reminds him you always have an opportunity to get a hit a fastball. She also gives two instances where a there's walk and a run scores.

Brody says he'll save that last pitch for later because he's not ready for the end."

"Brody!" Angela's voice startles him. "What are you doing? You're ten minutes late for the meeting."

He looks up at her with a huge grin. "I'm sorry. I was tied up."

"Yeah, right? You probably dozed off. Come on, because everyone's waiting for you."

"Did you book me for the cabin yet?" Brody asks.

"Not yet, because I thought I would do it next week after you return from your California trip."

"Good idea."

No more messages come by the end of the day, so Brody decides to message Searching for a Friend after dinner. He tells her he has a question for her. She accuses him of beginning the questioning, but Brody assures her it is just one question.

He asks why she wants to be just friends. Searching for a Friend replies she has trust issues with men. Brody wants to be honest with this woman and replies that he has trust issues with women. He waits for a response, but none comes. Shortly he sees she is offline.

Well, I have trust issues with women; he thinks. I've never married but have been engaged twice. The first engagement was broken off because she decided she didn't love me anymore if she ever did. The second was because my fiancé was only after my money.

Chapter 9

MADISON

Madison returns home Wednesday at lunchtime. The trip to Denver was a success; now, she has a lot of work. So, after checking in with Bridgette and unpacking, Madison works. She wants to get as much done as possible because she leaves again on Sunday for her next consulting job.

"I guess Lonesome Guy didn't like what I said because I haven't heard from him, but then again, I haven't checked for any messages," Madison says aloud, sitting at her desk and opening her laptop. It surprises her to see a message waiting for her.

"I prefer to ask my twenty questions when I meet a person. I like to look into their eyes to see if they give me honest answers."

"I can relate and agree," Madison responds, waiting for an answer that doesn't come. Staring at the laptop, it takes a few seconds for her to realize her cell phone is ringing. She picks it up, noticing the call is coming in on the cabin rental number.

"Pineville Wilderness Cabin. This is Madison Donaldson. May I help you?"

"Ms. Donaldson, my name is Angela Burrows. I want to make a reservation for my boss in your cabin. Could you tell me what your next available weekend is?"

"Ms. Burrows, please give me a second to grab my calendar." Madison grabs her calendar quickly. "Thank you for holding. Unfortunately, this weekend is booked, but I have had a cancellation for the following weekend. What days are you interested?"

"My boss would like to arrive Friday afternoon and leave early Monday morning. Is that possible?"

"Yes, those days are available. May I have your boss's name and how many in his party?"

"His name is Brody McGuire, and he will travel alone. Let me give you his credit card information."

Madison takes down the information and says, "Ms. Burrows, may I give you the reservation website in the event Mr. McGuire would like to stay again?"

"Thank you, but Mr. McGuire prefers I make his reservations in person, so there is no misunderstanding. He also prefers not to be bothered while he is there."

"I can appreciate that. There will be no contact made unless Mr. McGuire requires help. There is a secure gate. Let me give you the code; the key will be under the doormat. Thank you for calling. I hope Mr. McGuire will enjoy his stay."

After hanging up, Madison makes a note to talk to Perry about the website. Unfortunately, people are calling to make reservations instead of using it. That's fine because Madison enjoys talking to potential guests, but it requires extra work processing their credit cards. Thank goodness Mr. McGuire is suitable for that weekend. The cancellation was disappointing.

The rest of the week goes by quickly. Madison spends most of her time on her work, stopping to tend to the cabin as needed. She stops by Bruce's office and offers Bridgette a job working at the cabin when she is away. Bridgette is excited and happy to have the extra money. Madison informs Bridgette that she is leaving again on Sunday and will be back Tuesday. Next, she stops by Bruce's house and discusses the website with Perry. They decide to change from still pictures to scrolling videos showing the cabin, inside and out, the pond, and the beautiful scenery.

Unfortunately, no messages come from Lonesome Guy, which disappoints Madison, but she doesn't dwell on it. She has a lot to do before she leaves on Sunday for Nashville.

Chapter 10

MADISON

Madison is exhausted when she returns home Tuesday night from Nashville. She showers and gets a glass of wine before sitting on the sofa. Madison remembers she hasn't had time to check the singles website to see if Lonesome Guy has messaged her or if there are any new prospects. Pulling her laptop from her bag, she opens the website to find a message.

"Hi, Looking for a Friend. Sorry I haven't been in touch, but I was out of the state on business."

Madison stares at the message momentarily and then responds. *"No explanation needed and no apology necessary."*

"You intrigue me so much that I want to meet you. I live in Knoxville and will travel wherever I need to meet you."

"Is this your fastball?" Madison replies.

"LOL!!!! No, this is a slider. Will you meet me?"

"I live in Pineville. Do you know where that is?"

"Of course. I've been through there many times. I even had to stop at the only red light in town once."

"Well, it's been a while since you've been here because we now have two red lights."

"Is that a yes?"

"It's a yes. How is Saturday night at 7:00 at Vincent's Italian Restaurant?" Madison answers.

"Great, and I love Italian food. I look forward to it. How will I know you?"

"I'll be the only woman without a date." Madison adds a winking emoji and sends the message. She receives a thumbs-up emoji in response. This should be interesting, Madison says as she raises her glass to the ceiling in salute.

Friday at noon, Madison's cell phone rings with an incoming call on the cabin's line. "Pineville Wilderness Cabin. This is Madison Donaldson. May I help you?"

"Ms. Donaldson, this is Angela Burrows, Mr. McGuire's assistant." Madison holds her breath, waiting to hear a disappointing cancellation request. "Mr. McGuire will run late because of an unexpected meeting, so he probably won't arrive until around 9:00 pm. Will that be a problem?"

Madison exhales with a sigh of relief. "No problem, Ms. Burrows. Thank you for letting me know."

"My pleasure. Oh, and Mr. McGuire is looking forward to the stay and says he will post a review."

"I would appreciate the review and any suggestions Mr. McGuire may have. By the way, does Mr. McGuire have a special drink he prefers? After driving, he may like a drink to relax."

"That's very thoughtful of you, and I know he will appreciate it. He drinks Kentucky bourbon, of course. Any will do."

"Thank you for the information and for calling."

"Thank goodness," Madison says aloud once she disconnects the call. "I bet Mr. McGuire will forget to stop and get something to eat. I'll pick up a few things after I go to the liquor store."

Madison works until 7:00. She makes a quick sandwich for herself and two for Mr. McGuire. Then Madison goes by the liquor store and stops at the food store before heading to the cabin. She is bending over to put the cold items in the fridge when she hears the door open. She jumps, hitting her head on the door of the refrigerator.

"Are you okay?" a deep, grumpy voice asks.

Madison rubs her head and turns around. "Mr. McGuire?"

"Yes?"

"I'm Madison Donaldson. I was going to be gone by the time you got here. I apologize."

"I thought something was strange when I saw the gate open. What are you doing here? I thought I was going to be alone this weekend," Mr. McGuire asks in an exasperated voice.

"You were, and you will. I just assumed you might have forgotten to stop and buy some food. So I brought you some breakfast items and a bottle of bourbon."

Mr. McGuire stares down at the floor and runs his hands through his salt-and-pepper hair, giving Madison time to gaze at him. My God, he's gorgeous, she thinks. His long dark eyelashes brush the tops of his cheeks, and a light beard covers his firm jaw. Mr. McGuire is wearing a white dress shirt with the sleeves rolled up, giving Madison a glimpse of muscular, tanned forearms. Her eyes travel down his expansive chest to the gray slacks hugging his tampered hips and then to his feet, covered by expensive leather loafers.

When Mr. McGuire looks up at her, Madison blushes and sees the bluest eyes she has ever seen. They are dark blue like the Gulf of Alaska water and just as cold. "Ms. Donaldson, I apologize. It has been a long day, and I forgot to stop. I appreciate your thoughtfulness."

"Mr. McGuire, I also brought you a couple of sandwiches and chips as well, in case you're hungry."

"Thank you. I'm starving."

"Okay. I'll be on my way." Then, pointing to the list of rules lying on the counter, Madison says, "Mr. McGuire, it's not on the list, but if you like to fish, there is a storage room on the deck. There's a variety of fishing equipment in there. I keep it locked, but the key hangs over the front door. Well, good night, and enjoy your stay. My number is on the list if you need anything, day or night."

When she reaches the door, Madison turns to take a last admiring last look at Mr. McGuire and blushes again to find him looking at her.

"Ms. Donaldson, thank you again for your thoughtfulness."

Madison nods and leaves the cabin. Once in her car, she holds a deep breath and remembers the deep blue eyes. The eyes were tired, but there appeared to be sadness in them as well. "Not my problem," Madison says as she turns the car around and drives away.

Chapter 11

BRODY

"I am so freaking tired. Where is that entrance?" Brody says, talking to himself. "I should have left earlier to get here in the daylight. But no, that idiot from Western Technology just had to meet late this afternoon. I would have refused if I wasn't planning to buy his company."

Brody yawns and continues his conversation with himself. "This has been two endless weeks—a trip to California last week that video could have been done by and back-to-back meetings this week. I'm glad Angela suggested this getaway. It should be the break I need to start fresh next week. Now, if only I could find the entrance."

Driving slowly on the winding road, Brody's thoughts are interrupted by the GPS in his pickup. "You are approaching your destination on the left in 500 feet."

"Finally," Brody says. "Wait! The gate is open. Angela said the woman assured her I would be alone here. I hope the cabin wasn't double booked." Brody drives up the narrow path and sees lights on in the cabin with an SUV parked in the front.

Already tired and now upset, Brody leaves the pickup and marches up to the door. He quietly turns the knob and throws the door open to find a woman bent over with her head in the fridge. Brody only hears her head hitting the door because his eyes are fixed on the tight jeans covering her behind.

Using his grumpiest voice, Brody asks, "are you okay?"

The woman turns around as she rubs her head. Brody is startled by the emerald green eyes that meet his as she says, "Mr. McGuire?"

"Yes?" he answers in the same grumpy voice. The woman introduces herself and explains she was planning to be gone by the time he arrived. She also apologizes, barely registering in Brody's mind as he eyes the woman standing in front of him from head to toe. Her polo shirt is tucked into the waistband of her jeans, showing off a remarkable figure.

Brody tells her the gate was open, and he was concerned. He thought he would be alone. The woman explains she brought some food and bourbon.

Embarrassed from staring, Brody looks down at the floor. He runs his hands through his hair, trying to gather his thoughts. Finally, after a few seconds, Brody looks up at the woman and remembers his manners. He apologizes and thanks her. The woman adds she brought sandwiches and chips too. Brody thinks this woman is a gift from God but tells her he's hungry instead.

Brody hears her words when she tells him she's leaving but can't take his eyes off the woman. She's about five foot seven inches tall with shoulder-length silver hair. When she points to the list of rules, Brody's eyes are forced to follow her small but strong hand. He hears her say something about fishing equipment, a storage room, a key, and her phone number.

Brody's eyes follow her every movement as the woman goes to the door. She is graceful and walks with purpose, showing off her self-confidence. And there are those tight jeans covering her behind again. She turns and blushes when she reaches the door, noticing Brody's stare.

Rubbing his head to clear his mind, Brody thanks her again, and the woman nods and leaves. Brody doesn't move until he hears the SUV drive off. He walks over to the table and opens the fresh bottle of bourbon. Brody raises the bottle to his lips, not bothering with the glass the woman left beside the bottle. After a few gulps, he sits down and opens the chips and sandwiches the woman left for him.

As he eats, Brody looks at the items on the table. "It's as if the woman knows me," he thinks aloud. "My favorite bourbon, chips, and sandwiches. This whole situation is so strange."

Brody finishes his meal, gets ice out of the freezer, and pours some bourbon over the ice. Then, he walks around the cabin, admiring the various landscapes decorating the walls. The main bedroom is a pleasant surprise with a king-size bed. The ensuite has a huge walk-in shower, a built-in bench, and a rainforest showerhead.

"This is not what I was expecting at all," Brody says aloud. "I was expecting rustic, but this feels like a home. It is very warm and inviting." Next, he returns to the living room and opens the French doors. Finally, Brody steps out onto a large deck with lounge chairs illuminated by the three-quarters moon. Very nice, but I'm ready for bed," Brody yawns.

Although he didn't set an alarm, Brody wakes at 5:30. Lying in bed, he remembers the woman said there was fishing equipment. He saw a picture of a large pond a short distance from the cabin. I haven't been fishing since I was a kid. Brody thinks that sounds like fun and should help me relax. He gets up and dresses. I wonder where I can buy fishing bait this early.

Brody walks to the kitchen and retrieves the list of rules. He sees the woman's name and phone number at the very bottom. "Well, she said to call if I needed anything," Brody says and shrugs. After making a quick breakfast from the items the woman was kind enough to supply, Brody gives the woman a call.

The phone rings three times before a sleepy woman's voice answers hello.

"Ms. Donaldson, did I wake you?"

"That's okay, Mr. McGuire," the sleepy voice replies.

"I apologize. I assumed you would get ready for church at this hour." Brody catches himself smiling when he hears the woman snort into the phone.

"Mr. McGuire, you assume wrong. The church's pastor was concerned about the roof's structural integrity and demanded another parishioner take my place on the back pew." The comment causes Brody to bellow out an uncontrolled laugh. Good looks and a sense of humor, he thinks as the woman laughs with him. "Mr. McGuire, I know a couple of churches I can recommend for you that have an outstanding potluck today if you want to know about lunch prospects."

"Ms. Donaldson, I think I can manage lunch on my own," Brody replies, still laughing. "I was calling to ask where I can buy worms and minnows."

"That doesn't sound very appetizing for lunch. However, once you get on the highway back to town, there is a convenience store about two miles down the road with what you need, including cornmeal and cooking oil."

"Thank you for the information. I'll try not to bother you again," Brody says back in his grumpy voice.

"No problem, Mr. McGuire. Good luck with your fishing." The woman hangs up without waiting for a reply.

Good gosh, why did I have to sound grumpy? Brody asks himself. The woman made me laugh hard, which I hadn't done in forever. He heads to the store, returning with his minnows and worms.

After fishing all day, Brody stops and cleans up for his dinner date with Searching for a Friend. I hope this dinner is the perfect ending to a perfect day, he ponders as he dresses in black jeans and a navy button-down shirt. Then, after pulling his boots on, he grabs his laptop and sends a quick message.

37

Chapter 12

MADISON

After spending all day trying to decide what to wear for her dinner with Lonesome Guy, Madison decides on a simple, short-sleeved green cotton dress and sandals. This isn't a date, she reminds herself as she looks in the full-length mirror. But, *you wish it were*, the woman in the mirror replies, making Madison frown.   "Shall we have dinner now?" Madison nods. Brody offers his arm to her, and they walk back into the restaurant together. The tingling sensation happens again, confusing Madison even more.

A message pings on Madison's laptop as she walks to the door. She opens the message and is pleased to see it is from Lonesome Guy. *"I can't wait to meet you,"* the message says.

"That makes two of us," Madison says aloud as she walks out the door.

She walks into the restaurant at 6:50. Madison's ten minutes early and looks around to see if any unattached men are milling around. Not seeing any, she heads to the bar, not paying attention to any of the patrons.

"Ms. Donaldson, what a pleasant surprise."

Shocked, Madison looks to her right and sees Mr. McGuire sitting at the bar. "Hi, Mr. McGuire. Please call me Madison. Ms. Donaldson was my mother."

"Okay, Madison, but please call me Brody. Are you meeting someone?" Madison nods. "Can I buy you a drink while you wait?"

"That would be nice. I'll have a glass of red wine, please." Madison continues to scan the bar and restaurant but sees no one that could be her date.

"Please have a seat," Brody tells her, motioning toward the vacant stool next to him. "I promise I don't bite."

Madison smiles and sits down. "How was your fishing expedition today?" she asks.

"It was great and so relaxing. The pond and surrounding area are beautiful. The cabin is beautiful. I was expecting something more rustic, but it feels so homey."

"I'm glad you're happy. It is a beautiful place."

Madison and Brody continue talking for several minutes while Madison scans the bar and restaurant. Finally, she looks at her watch, and it says 7:15. "Well, Brody, it appears my dinner date threw me a curve ball and decided not to show up. So I think I'll go. Enjoy the rest of your stay and thank you for the drink." Madison stands and walks away when she feels a warm but strong hand on her arm.

"Madison, are you searching for a friend?"

Madison swings around and glares at Brody, shaking his hand away. "Mr. McGuire, how dare you to assume I'm that type of woman." She quickly turns and almost runs to the exit.

"Madison, wait," Brody says, trying to catch up to her. Madison pretends not to hear and keeps walking quickly. As she gets to her car and opens her door, the warm, muscular hand is placed on top of hers. A tingling sensation runs up her arm, momentarily confusing her, and she jerks her hand away.

"Madison, please wait and let me explain," Brody says, sounding earnest.

"Then, start explaining because I don't have all night," she demands.

Brody backs up, giving Madison space. "I was supposed to meet a woman here tonight at 7:00. I met her on a dating app. She goes by the name Looking for a Friend. Since my date and yours didn't show, I wondered if you might be her."

"Oh, my gosh! Are you Lonesome Guy from Knoxville?"

Brody grins from ear to ear. "I am, so can we start tonight over?" Madison smiles. "Hi! I'm Brody McGuire, AKA Lonesome Guy from Knoxville." He reaches his hand out to her.

"Hello, Brody. I'm Madison Donaldson, AKA Searching for a Friend. It's nice to meet you," she shakes his hand.

Chapter 13

BRODY

While they wait for their table, Brody thinks back a few moments to the angry eyes of Madison Donaldson. The parking lot's lights captured the depth of her emerald eyes, captivating him. I bet she's a spitfire underneath that soft exterior. Having her as a friend with no strings attached might be fun. I need to find out if she likes me for me or me for my money, like all the other women I know.

Once seated and their orders placed, Brody says, "I'm glad we got that straightened out, and I'm happy you're Searching for a Friend."

"Me, too," Madison replies shyly. "Shall we get to know each other? I'll let you start with the interrogation." She gives Brody her best smile.

"Okay. Tell me about the cabin. As I said, it feels like home."

"My parents bought the land before I was born, and my dad built the cabin himself. Then, they left it to my brother and me when they died. I lived there for a couple of years until a few months ago when I bought a house in town. I bought my brother out and decided to rent it out as a vacation home."

"No wonder it feels like home because it has your touch all over it."

Madison blushes. "Well, mine and my mother's. I didn't change everything." Finally, their food arrives, and the pair continues to talk through dinner.

"Why did you move?" Brody asks, studying her face. "The cabin seems more suitable for you."

"Well, technology isn't as good in the rural areas, and I needed a better internet connection for the cabin rental."

"Your profile said you do consulting work as well," Brody remarks, not wanting to appear too nosy. Madison nods her head. Throughout dinner, Madison waves at various people behind Brody. "You seem to know several people."

"Yes, I know many since I grew up here."

"Have you always lived here?"

"No, I had to move several times for my work."

"Well, if it isn't Madison Johnson. Sorry, I meant Donaldson," a loud voice says. Madison and Brody both turn in the man's direction's voice.

"Wyatt," Madison says in an exasperated voice.

"Robbing the cradle, old girl?" the man asks.

"You should know, Wyatt. You're the expert," Madison replies with a sharp edge to her voice. "Wyatt, this is my friend Brody. Brody, this is Wyatt."

"Wyatt," a shrill voice yells. All three turn in the voice's direction as a young twenty-ish woman walks up.

"I told you to wait at the table for me," Wyatt says harshly to the woman.

"Oh honey, I was, but I have to go potty. Hi, Madison."

"Hi, Cheryl. This is Brody. Brody, this is Cheryl, Wyatt's wife." Brody and Cheryl nod at each other. "Cheryl, I didn't know you were expecting," Madison says with a touch of amusement in her voice.

"Oh, Madison, isn't it wonderful? Wyatt and I will have a bouncing bundle of joy in two more months. Of course, Wyatt wishes for a boy, but I don't care as long as it's healthy," Cheryl replies.

"Of course, Wyatt is hoping for a boy," Madison says with a smirk. "After five girls, he needs a boy to carry on the Johnson name and inherit the ranch. Don't you, Wyatt?"

Wyatt's face turns red in a flash of anger, and he clenches his fists at his sides. "Cheryl, I thought you said you had to go to the bathroom. Go! I'll be in the car." Wyatt turns abruptly and stomps off in the exit's direction. Cheryl gives a little wave and walks toward the restrooms.

"Ex-husband," Madison says, looking down at her plate.

"Not a fan of his, are you?" Brody asks.

Madison looks directly into his eyes. "What gave you that idea?"

Brody shrugs. "How long have you two been divorced?"

"Forty years. No, I'm not married, and I'm not in a relationship of any kind before you ask," Madison says, staring intensely into his dark blue eyes.

"I would not ask. You said you have trust issues. I remember that and everything else you said. I've never been married. I was engaged twice. Once, she broke it off, and the other time I did. I don't do relationships because I don't have time."

"And you have trust issues, too. We make a fine pair, don't we?" Madison says with a laugh. "It's getting late, and I need to be going. Thank you for dinner. It was a pleasure to meet you, Lonesome Guy from Knoxville."

"Let me pay the check, and I'll walk you to your car," Brody says, signaling the waitress.

When they arrive at Madison's car, Brody takes her hands. "Madison, I like you, and I know I have to earn your trust. I think we might be good friends. I'm not good at messages and emails. I prefer to talk to people in person. I want to talk to you again. If you're not busy tomorrow, I'll be watching football all afternoon and would like you to join me."

"Brody, I like you too. I'll come tomorrow under one condition. You let me come before noon and bring snacks. We can watch football and eat all day without worrying about lunch or dinner."

"I like that idea. Come whenever you get ready. I'll be down at the pond if I'm not at the house. Thank you for tonight." Brody squeezes her hands before turning to go to his pickup.

Chapter 14

BRODY

"Well, that was a delightful evening," Brody says aloud while buckling his seat belt. Then, not wanting to miss the cabin, he sets the GPS and leaves the restaurant. His mind wanders to Madison, but Brody shakes his head to clear his thoughts. He needs to pay attention to his driving and watch for wildlife.

Once at the cabin, Brody pours himself a bourbon and relaxes on the deck to enjoy the mild evening. His mind returns to Madison and dinner. There are obviously hard feelings between Madison and her ex-husband, even if it had been forty years. There's an important story there, he ponders. That may be what started her trust issues.

Brody swirls the soothing dark liquid over the ice cubes as he stares at the mountain in front of him. He remembers their dinner conversation. Madison answered his questions, but Brody felt there was more than what she told him. She didn't ask him questions, which was odd. I'll ask her about that tomorrow.

Laying his head back on the lounge chair, Brody thinks about Madison herself. She is a beautiful woman with an impressive figure. That may be why the town now has two red lights so travelers can glimpse the beautiful woman as they pass through. Brody smiles at the thought. Madison is unaware of her beauty, he decides. She never noticed the appreciative looks of the men and some women who looked in her direction at the restaurant.

Brody stands and returns to the kitchen to refill his glass. He looks around and remembers Madison's thoughtfulness when she brought the food and bourbon last night. I feel she is a very caring person who is very guarded about who and what she cares about. Obviously, she cares deeply about this cabin, but something more than the Wi-Fi made her decide to move to town.

Once the drink is poured, Brody returns to the deck and stands at the railing. Could he be friends with Madison? Could they have fun and enjoy each other's company, or would it get complicated and ruin any possibility of friendship? Or does she know who he is and will be after the prestige he has in the business world and his money? I guess time will tell.

After a good night's sleep, Brody is up early and on his way to the pond as the sun rises. He tries not to think about Madison, but the sun hits the pond's water just right, reminding him of her emerald eyes and how dark they turned when she assumed he thought she was a whore. Brody smiles and admits he is looking forward to seeing Madison today. The fish are biting, and Brody loses all track of time when he suddenly hears a soft voice behind him.

"Having any luck?"

"Madison, hi. I'm having excellent luck. How are you today?"

"I'm great. Are you about to finish up since the kick-off between the Giants and Jets is thirty minutes away?"

"Wow! Is it that time already?" Madison gives Brody a huge grin and nods. "I need to get this stuff together and back to the cabin. I need a shower, too, before the game starts."

"Here, let me help you," Madison says, reaching for the unused fishing equipment.

"Madison, do you fish?"

"No, I don't have the patience for it, and I hate the taste of fish."

Brody laughs and says, "that's good to know," as he gathers up the rest of the fishing equipment.

The pair walks to the cabin in silence. "I'll put this stuff away while you shower," Madison says when they reach the cabin.

"Thanks. I won't be long."

On the path back to the cabin, he noticed Madison was wearing a t-shirt and capris, so casual dress is the style of the day, Brody decides. He showers quickly and dresses in jeans and a t-shirt.

"That was fast," Madison says as Brody walks into the kitchen. "Are you hungry?"

"I am. I was so interested in getting an early start I forgot to eat breakfast. It smells wonderful in here. What did you bring to eat?" Brody asks, walking over to the table where Madison has the snacks laid out.

"Well, I have cheese dip and guacamole, sausage balls, wings, veggies with ranch dressing, and chips, of course. There's fruit and cookies for dessert. I didn't know if you're a beer drinker, but I brought a six-pack just in case."

"Madison, this is perfect," Brody says, walking beside her. "Thank you." Before he realizes what he is doing, Brody places a soft kiss on her cheek, which catches her off guard. Madison backs away, wearing a surprised look. "I'm sorry. I just wanted to show my appreciation."

"It's okay. I'm not used to it, is all. Now, fill your plate because you have three minutes. Would you like a beer?"

"Yes, please," Brody answers as he piles his plate full of food. Once he sits down on the couch, Madison delivers his beer with a smile.

By the time she fills her plate and sits on the opposite end of the sofa, Brody is headed back to the table to refill his plate. "Madison, did you make all this?"

"Yep."

"You must be an excellent cook."

"I get by. Mac and cheese is my specialty, though." Brody sits down and stares at her. "What, Brody? Did I say something wrong?"

"Mac and cheese is my favorite food. My housekeeper makes it for me with plenty of leftovers once a week." Oh no, Brody thinks. I just told Madison I have a housekeeper. He notices she appears to ignore his comment.

"I bet mine is better. It's my mom's recipe," Madison says. "Maybe I'll make it for you sometime."

"I'd like that. Can you talk and watch the game?"

Madison grins at Brody. "Of course. I don't particularly like either of these teams. The Packers are my favorite."

Brody looks at Madison in surprise. "Mine too."

"Yeah, I fell in love with the team when I watched the first Super Bowl."

Brody notices a sudden change in Madison's facial expression and her demeanor. "Madison," he says softly. "I don't care about your age if that worries you. Genuine friends don't care about things like that." When Madison doesn't look at him, Brody reaches over and lifts her chin to see into her eyes.

"Brody, I'm not trying to hide my age. You can easily tell by looking at me I'm older than you."

"Age is a number. It's how you feel and act that matters. Remember that. Now, I have a question for you," Brody says as he moves his hand back to his plate. "Why didn't you ask me questions last night?"

Madison sits quietly for a few seconds. "Well, I rarely ask many questions. People can tell me what they want. I listen and watch their eyes and faces. I'm good at reading between the lines, watching body movements, and determining the truth. I have found that I'm much more likely to be lied to if I ask questions. I always try to look for the good in people."

"Hmmm. Madison, do you know who I am and what I do?"

"If you're asking me if I researched you on the internet or social media, the answer is no. I don't do that. All I know is that your name is Brody McGuire, and you work in technology. You live in Knoxville, attend social events only out of necessity, and have a housekeeper. Based on what you've told me, I assume you live in an apartment because you seem to enjoy the outdoors here so much. However, you work many hours, and your job is stressful. Now, I know you love the Packers and mac and cheese. Is there anything else you would like me to know?"

Brody can't help but laugh, which makes Madison laugh. "Well, let's see what I can come up with. I was born in a small town much like this one. We lived there until I was eight when my dad died. After that, my mother and I moved to Bowling Green. My mother went to work for a car dealership and married the owner. Now, she is a wealthy woman who travels the world with her rich husband. How's that?"

"I'm sorry about your dad."

"I'm not. He was a mean drunk who liked to take his anger out on my mother and me. My mother worked three jobs while he would lie around the house and drink. I tried to help my mother by caring for the house and cooking, although there wasn't much to eat. I guess what I'm trying to tell you is that I never really got to experience small-town life. I've been curious about it, which led me to rent the cabin when I saw it on the internet. Your turn, Madison."

"Okay. My parents, brother, and I were born and raised here. My brother is two years older than I am. Three years after high school, my brother moved to Seattle. He only came back to our parents' funerals. I got married out of high school, divorced, and got a job with a bank. Do you have any siblings?"

"No, I don't," Brody says. "Are you and your brother close?"

"No, we never talk except when he told me how much he wanted for his share of the cabin."

"I can read between the lines as well, Madison. You married Wyatt right out of high school."

"Yeah. He and my brother were best friends, so I grew up with him."

Brody gets up and carries his plate to the kitchen. He looks over at Madison, who is staring at the TV. Brody thinks about Madison's interaction with her ex last night. Somehow, her brother is involved in the story as well. "Do you have any dear friends?" he asks.

"I have a best friend, Bruce, that I grew up with. He is my financial advisor and lives here with his partner. We were inseparable in school and college. Do you have any close friends?"

"Well, there's Ted, who I met while we were in college. He's single and lives and works in Knoxville. We play golf occasionally and poker once a week with a few other acquaintances. Ted is more interested in his social life, especially which woman he can get into bed with, than hanging out with me. He's not one I feel I can confide in or totally trust."

"Sounds like a great guy," Madison says sarcastically.

"Ted's okay. He changed after college. We have different priorities in life now. His are women, and mine is work."

"Sounds boring for you."

"It is sometimes. That's why I'm Lonesome Guy in Knoxville, looking for a good friend." Brody walks over to Madison and takes her hand in his. "Madison, will you be my friend?"

Madison squeezes his hand, ignoring the tingling feeling, and gives Brody a big smile. "Yes, Lonesome Guy. I'll be your friend," she answers, standing. "I have to warn you I'm a hugger."

"Me, too," Brody says, pulling her into his arms and holding her tightly. "Thank you, Madison," he whispers in her ear. It makes the hair on the back of her neck stand at attention, and a warm feeling runs down the length of her body.

"Okay, let's not get too sappy," she pulls away quickly, laughing as she does. "The Packers are getting ready to kick off."

Chapter 15

MADISON

This was an interesting day, Madison thinks as she crawls into bed. Maybe Brody and I can be friends. We both like the Packers and yelling at the referees, players, and coaches during the game. We both like mac and cheese and the cabin. Brody is very considerate and well-mannered, which tells me his mom raised him well. And he is so dang handsome. But wait, that will not work. If we're going to be friends, I need to keep those thoughts out of my head. Madison turns over, falling asleep quickly, dreaming of dark blue eyes, salt and pepper hair, and broad shoulders.

The following day, Madison is neck-deep at work when her laptop pings with a note from Brody.

"Thanks for a wonderful day yesterday. Is the cabin available for next weekend?"

"You are welcome. I enjoyed the day as well. Sorry, it's unavailable."

There are a few minutes of silence before Brody replies. *"I would like to see you again if you're interested and not busy next weekend. What are some excellent hotels in the area?"*

Madison smiles at the response. *"I would love to see you again as well. But, unfortunately, all the local hotels are booked because of the county fair."*

"That's very disappointing."

Thinking back on the conversation she and Brody had yesterday, Madison has an idea. *"You are welcome to stay at the cabin, but there are three conditions."*

Brody responds immediately. *"Strings attached already? Hmmm. I don't know about that so tell me your conditions."*

"Condition #1—You have to share the cabin with me. I'm having some work done in my house and have to move out for a few days."

"I can live with that," Brody replies.

"Condition #2—You must let me plan the activities for Saturday." Madison smiles when she presses send. I know exactly what I want to do.

"Scary, but I'll agree."

"Condition #3—you be my plus one at a black-tie fundraising event the following weekend." Madison presses send and thinks, why did I do that? Because a good-looking man that no one knows as your plus one is a good thing for this town.

Several minutes go by without a response. Then a message arrives. *"Sorry, I had to check my social calendar, and I just happen to be free that weekend to attend a dull fundraising event. I agree with all your conditions. Is it really a black tie?"*

Madison laughs and checks her calendar. *"Yes, but as an added incentive, you get a free weekend at the cabin."*

"And here I thought the only advantage to being a plus one was to see you all dressed up. So black tie it is, and I'll try not to embarrass you in front of your friends," Brody says.

"Thank goodness. I was really concerned about that, and just an FYI. I do like to dance if you need to brush up. Please let me know

what time you plan to arrive on Friday. If it's early enough, there may be mac and cheese on the menu."

"That's enough of an incentive to arrive by dinner time. Thanks and have a pleasant week."

"I hope you do too."

Chapter 16

BRODY

"Brody. Brody! Earth to Brody," Angela says, walking into his office. Brody's back is to her, staring out the window. When he still doesn't acknowledge that he's heard her, Angela touches him on the shoulder. Brody jumps and turns around. "Brody, where are you today?"

"I'm standing here, aren't I?"

"Well, physically, you're here, but your mind has been elsewhere all day. You said you had a good time at the cabin, but I wonder if that was true." Angela walks over and sits in Brody's chair.

"Angela, I believe that's my chair."

"Oh yeah. So it is. You can sit in the other one," she points to the chair on the opposite side of the desk.

"You're fired, you know that, don't you?" Brody asks with a serious expression.

"Okay, but who's going to run this company while you're off in La-La Land? Oh, never mind. I'm fired, so I'll get my purse and go," Angela says but remains seated, staring at her boss and crossing her arms.

The two stare at each other for several seconds before Angela says, "are you going to tell me what's going on?"

"Don't you have work to do?" Brody glares at her.

"I do, but my boss is a pushover," Angela replies with a grin.

Brody sighs. "Okay, here goes. I got to the cabin late, and the woman you made the reservation with was there. She was very thoughtful and brought food and bourbon, assuming I would forget to stop and buy food, which I did."

"That was very nice of her. She asked me what you liked to drink when I made the reservation."

"The second part of the story is that the dating app matched me with a woman based on my profile. We communicated a little. I liked what she had to say, and I said I wanted to meet her. She told me she lives in Pineville, so I arranged to meet her last Saturday night for dinner."

Angela studies Brody's face as he talks. "Brody, isn't Pineville where the cabin is?"

"Yeah. Long story short, the woman from the cabin is my match from the dating app."

"Wow! Isn't it a small world? Well, how was it?" Angela asks, watching Brody's reactions.

"The cabin was fantastic, and the woman was even better."

"Please, please tell me you didn't sleep with her."

Brody laughs. "No, it's not like that. Neither of us wants that type of relationship. We are both just looking for a friend to hang out with. She's beautiful inside and out. We have a lot in common, it seems. I'm going back this weekend."

"Really? For her or the cabin?" Angela smirks.

"Both, I guess. The pond is great for fishing, and I'd like to get to know this woman better. Her name is Madison, but you already know that. I'm also going back the following weekend. She asked me to be her plus one at a fundraiser."

"Brody, you're not getting ahead of yourself, are you?"

"No, it's just that she is so different from any other woman I know. She's retired but does consultation work. Madison owns the cabin and a house in town, so I feel she's financially stable."

"What kind of work did she do?"

"Madison said she worked in Human Resources for a bank. That's all I know."

"I'll check it out," Angela says. "She certainly sounds different from Lauren and those other piranhas you usually go out with. Now, your video conference starts in ten minutes. By the way, Ted called and canceled your poker game this week. He and two other guys will be out of town."

"Okay, thanks. Now, why don't you earn your paycheck," Brody says with a grin.

Chapter 17

BRODY

The following morning, Brody barely gets into his office before hearing the door closing behind him. He doesn't turn around. "That better be coffee, Angela," Brody says.

"Coffee and information," Angela replies, handing him a cup of his favorite coffee. "Sit down. I have so much to tell you." Brody rolls his eyes and sits down next to her.

"Let me guess. This has nothing to do with your job."

"Brody, you are my job, so listen up. I talked to Nancy in HR. I told her you met Madison Donaldson, and she got so excited. Nancy said Ms. Donaldson is the foremost authority on all things related to Human Resources. She served as president of the national organization three times. Ms. Donaldson has written many articles published in highly regarded magazines and journals. She is a speaker every year at national and international conferences. Nancy has heard her speak many times. Nancy also said that she read that Ms. Donaldson had retired but was doing consulting work. Currently, she is working with two Fortune 100 companies."

"Wow," Brody says. "That's impressive." He rubs his chin.

"Nancy hopes if we ever have a severe problem, you might hire Ms. Donaldson. I also researched the fundraiser. Ms. Donaldson is a co-chair, and the fundraiser is to benefit the county's humane society. So, in other words, Brody, you have found an intelligent friend who doesn't need your money or status. There is one thing, though."

"What's that?"

"She's older than you are," Angela says quietly.

"I already know that, Angela. I'm looking for a friend, not a wife. Now, thanks for the information. After I fire you, you can get a job as a private investigator. Don't I have a meeting soon?"

"Oh, Brody. I know you love me," Angela says, standing and walking toward the door. "I'm always here for advice."

Brody throws his napkin at her as she opens the door to leave. He shakes his head and goes to stand by the windows. Wow, that was a lot of information Angela shared. I won't let Madison know, but it gives me some insight into her life. Brody takes his phone out of his pocket. He downloaded the app to his phone last night to access Madison and their messages easier. He sends her a message saying he is looking forward to the weekend.

Chapter 18

MADISON

By the time Friday rolls around, Madison has almost completed one of her jobs. She packs up her laptop and a suitcase of clothes to take to the cabin. The painters will be at the house early in the morning. The foreman picked up the key earlier, so Madison is free to leave now. As she climbs into her SUV, Madison realizes she is eager to see Brody tonight, but first, she has to stop by the food store.

While Madison is in the food store, Brody messages her he plans to arrive around 6:00 pm. That gives her four hours to get ready for him. First, since Brody is her guest, Madison places her things in the extra bedroom so he can have the master suite. Next, she washes and peels the apples for the apple crisp they will have for dessert. Then, Madison mixes the mac and cheese to stick in the oven later. Finally, she puts clean sheets on his bed and fresh linens in the bathroom.

Madison checks the time. She still has two hours, so she goes to the woodpile and gathers wood for the fire pit. Even though it is a warm evening, Madison decides sitting by the fire pit talking would be a pleasant change for Brody. Finished with that chore, she realizes she is getting nervous. Returning to the kitchen, Madison pours a glass of wine to soothe her nerves hopefully and places the apple crisp in the oven to bake. That gives her enough time to prepare the salad and the dressing.

The apple crisp comes out of the oven at 5:30, and the mac and cheese goes in. The cabin smells wonderful, Madison thinks. I hope Brody will like the food. Then, finally, she hears his pickup pull into the driveway. Madison gets a glass from the cabinet, puts ice in the glass, and pours the bourbon.

"My gosh, woman." Brody opens the door and says, "I can smell dinner outside. I was already hungry, but now I'm famished." He gives Madison a huge smile, making her heart flutter and chills run down her spine.

"I'm glad to hear that because there will be enough leftovers to take home with you," Madison replies with a wink.

"I detect the aroma of apples and cinnamon," he says, walking toward her.

"Dessert," Madison replies, handing him his drink. "We've got about twenty minutes before dinner's ready. Would you like to sit on the deck while we wait?"

"That sounds great, and thanks for the drink. After you," Brody says, motioning for Madison to go ahead.

She walks to the deck's railing and looks out over the mountain. "I never tire of this view," Madison says, walking over and lighting the fire pit.

"It is beautiful," Brody agrees, sitting down. The pair talks about their week until the timer on the oven goes off. Finally, Madison heads for the door. "Let me help you, Madison." Brody jumps up, holds the door for her, and follows her into the kitchen.

Brody sets the table while Madison places the food on it. When they sit down and finally are ready to eat, she holds her breath, waiting for

Brody to take his first bite of the mac and cheese. He takes a forkful, blows on it slightly to cool it, and then places it in his mouth.

"Madison, I have died and gone to mac and cheese heaven. This is the best I have ever tasted. What's your secret?" Brody says, taking another forkful.

She gives him her biggest smile. "Well, I used four different kinds of cheese to start. If you like it that much, I'll send the recipe to your housekeeper." Brody nods and continues to eat and eat and eat.

Finally, Madison says, "Brody, you should leave room for dessert." She gets up, retrieving the warm apple crisp and vanilla ice cream from the freezer.

"Did you make this too?"

"Well, not the ice cream," Madison laughs and begins serving them. "Why don't we eat around the fire pit?"

"Great idea if you'll help me out of my chair," Brody says, pretending to struggle to stand up. He reaches out his hand to Madison. She takes it, pulling harder than necessary. Brody leaps out of the chair simultaneously and crashes into her. Madison gasps as his body hits hers, not from the force but from the warmth. She looks at Brody and sees a spark of something in his blue eyes. He quickly backs away, apologizes, and reaches for his dessert. "Need any help with yours?" Brody asks with a gruffness in his voice. Madison replies no and follows him outside with her bowl.

Chapter 19

BRODY

As he helps Madison clean up the kitchen and put the food away, Brody tries to find out the agenda for the following day. However, Madison just said it was a surprise, and no matter what he said or did, she didn't give any hints. Instead, she said they needed to be home by 7:00 because the Packers play a Saturday night game.

When bedtime comes, Madison insists Brody take the master suite. He argues but loses. After grabbing his things from the pickup, Brody rests on the bed and looks around the room. What a fantastic night, he reflects. Madison is a superb cook, and sitting around the firepit talking was so relaxing. It was just what he needed.

The only awkward moment was when Brody inadvertently crashed into Madison. He didn't expect her to pull so hard on his hand. The feeling Brody got being so close to her was unexpected but very nice. Brody could see the uneasiness in Madison's eyes, so he backed away quickly.

Deciding he wants another bourbon before heading to bed, Brody goes into the kitchen only to run into a Madison clad in a towel. "Oh, sorry," he says. "I just wanted to get another drink before I turn in."

"It's me that should be sorry. I came after a bottle of water," Madison blushes, looking at the floor.

Brody gazes at the beautiful woman standing before him. The towel touches her right above the knees. Her skin looks so soft and warm from the top of her neck to where the towel wraps around her breasts. Brody clears his throat and walks around Madison. He pours his bourbon and walks back to the bedroom, not looking at her.

"Well, good night again," he says in a deep, throaty voice.

"Good night, Brody."

He closes the door, leans against it, and takes a deep breath. Madison really doesn't know how gorgeous she is. Just the thought of her in that towel makes his body react to her. I can't think of her that way, or else this friendship will not last. He downs the bourbon in one gulp and heads to bed.

Brody wakes to the smell of bacon. He showers, spending more time than he plans to, but he physically needs the release a part of his body demands. Dressed in jeans and a T-shirt, he walks into the kitchen. Madison is dressed in a robe and has her back to him as she faces the cooktop. "Good morning, Madison."

She turns around and smiles. "Good morning. How would you like your eggs, and how many?"

"Two over easy, please. Are these clothes okay for today?"

Madison looks at him from top to bottom. Then, turning back to the cooktop, she says, "the clothes are fine, but I think sneakers would be better than boots."

"Okay, I'll change. Do you need any help?"

"Nope, I'm good. The coffee is ready if you are."

Brody changes into sneakers and then pours his coffee as Madison sits the plate of bacon and eggs in front of him. The eggs are perfectly cooked. As the two people eat, they talk about general things. Finally, Brody cleans up the kitchen while Madison dresses.

The sight of Madison walking out of the bedroom dressed in a polo and jeans makes Brody catch his breath. She pulled her silver hair back into a ponytail, and her eyes sparkle. Madison is so secure about herself that she doesn't feel the need to wear makeup all the time, Brody believes. The women he knows wouldn't be caught dead without makeup, even to the point of sleeping in it.

"Ready to go?" she asks with a grin. Brody nods. "Great. I'm driving."

Fifteen minutes later, Madison pulls into a parking lot next to the county fairgrounds. She watches Brody looking out the window for a few moments. "Welcome to the county fair. After what you told me about your childhood, I bet you've never been. So Brody here's your chance to be a child."

"Madison, this is wonderful. Let's go." Brody gets out and hurries around the SUV to open the door for her. The parking lot is full of cars, and many people walk toward the gate. "Madison," Brody says, looking down at her. "Would it be okay to hold hands, so we don't get separated?"

She looks up at him and sees the earnestness on his face. "Of course, we can." Madison reaches out her hand to him. When Brody takes it, she feels a tingling run up her arm and down to her core. If he feels anything, he doesn't show it, Madison notices.

As they walk to the gate, Madison explains about the projects the kids have worked on. Steers, pigs, sheep, goats, and chickens are in the livestock barn. The women's building has pies, cakes, clothing, jams, and jellies. Madison also explains the judging of the projects and the auction to be held in the afternoon, where the items will be sold.

Brody listens intently and asks if they can attend the auction. Madison assures him they have plenty of time to do so. She tells him she usually bids on several items and sometimes wins the bidding.

First, the pair heads to the livestock barn, looking over all the animals and chickens. All the judging of the animals has already taken place. Some kids are with their animals, and Brody talks to several, asking questions that please Madison.

Next, they go to the women's building, where they sample a few jams and jellies. When they reach the clothing, Brody practically drags Madison to where an evening gown is displayed, sporting a blue ribbon for first place.

"Madison, that gown would look gorgeous on you," Brody says, pointing at the black, off-the-shoulder gown. She rolls her eyes.

The dressmaker overhears him and looks Madison over. "The dress is a size 12, but I can always take it up if you win it."

"Oh, she'll win it," Brody assures the girl. He looks down at Madison and smiles. Madison shakes her head but asks the girl how long it would take to alter the dress. The girl replies three days.

Next, the pair walks past the various food vendors as they leave the women's building. Brody inhales deeply and looks from side to side at all the choices available.

"Madison, I think I would like to try a turkey leg. Would you share one with me?"

She laughs and says, "okay, but I get to pick dessert." After purchasing a huge turkey leg and drinks, the pair finds a table and sits down to eat. Brody tears a piece of the leg and feeds it to Madison.

"Well, if it isn't the old woman and her boy toy," a familiar voice says. Madison and Brody turn toward the loud voice.

"Wyatt, how good to see you again," Madison says sarcastically.

Wyatt looks at Brody. "I can't believe you're still hanging around with someone older than you. There are so many good-looking women around to choose from."

Brody stands, and Madison places her hand on his arm. "Wyatt, I would appreciate you not speaking to Madison like that. She is a beautiful, kind woman who doesn't deserve your caustic comments."

"Oh, did I hit a nerve? Well, you don't know her as I do, but if you hang around long enough, you'll find out she can be a genuine witch." Wyatt turns and stomps off.

"You didn't have to do that," Madison states as Brody returns to his seat.

"Yes, I did. I don't like him talking to you like that. I know he's your ex, but that was long ago. What's the story behind his hate for you?"

"Brody, that's a story for another time. Let's not ruin the day. I've had enough turkey. I'm going to get our dessert." She stands and walks off toward several food vendors. Moments later, she returns with a plate piled high with stings of something topped with a white powder.

Madison sets the plate between her and Brody. "Have you ever had funnel cake?" Brody replies no. She smiles, reaches into her purse, and hands him a wet wipe. "It's a staple of fairs. You go first and pull off a piece."

Brody does as he's told and plops the bite into his mouth. He smiles and says, "that's delicious. I thought cotton candy was a staple. Can we have some later?" Madison laughs, nods, and takes a bite of the funnel cake.

When they finish eating, Brody takes Madison's hand and leads them to the amusement rides. They ride several smaller rides before approaching the Ferris wheel.

"Madison, I always wanted to ride a Ferris wheel. Would you ride it with me?" Brody asks, staring up at the wheel as it spins around slowly.

"No, Brody. I can't, but you go ahead. I'll stay here and watch."

Brody releases her hand and turns to her. "Please?"

"I can't, Brody," Madison says, looking at the ground.

Using his index finger, Brody lifts her chin to look into her eyes. "Why not?"

"I'm terrified of heights," she whispers, looking at him quickly and then looking down again.

"Madison, please look at me." She raises her eyes to look into his. "I will take care of you, I promise. Today and always," Brody says, brushing her cheek with his fingertips.

She puts her hand on top of his. "I know you think you can, but I just can't do this ride." She pulls his hand away from her cheek. "I want you to ride it, though. I'll stand right here and watch, I promise."

Brody nods slowly, turns, and buys a ticket to ride the Ferris wheel. Madison watches with a smile. I'm not sure how old Brody is, but today he is ten, Madison thinks as she watches him climb into the gondola and is strapped in.

As the Ferris wheel begins to turn and Brody is lifted higher in the air, Madison can hear him laugh. He spots her and waves. When Brody reaches the top of the wheel, it stops for a couple of minutes to let more people onto the ride.

Brody waves again and yells, "hey, Madison. Look at me. I'm on top of the world." He stands up, causing her to gasp, but he quickly sits back down. "I miss you," he yells to her with a massive grin. Madison laughs and waves at him, realizing his comment makes her feel warm all over.

Back on the ground, Brody rushes back to Madison. Full of adrenaline, he picks her up and swings her around. When he sits her down, Brody kisses her on the forehead before taking her hand and asking what's next.

Madison leads Brody to the games. He plays several and wins two small stuffed bears. One he gives to Madison and the other to a crying little girl in a stroller. She stops crying and gives Brody a big smile, which warms Madison's heart.

Madison carries her bear as if it were a precious gift, leading Brody to the auction barn. As they enter, she sees Bruce waving and patting the bench beside him.

"There are my friends, Bruce and Perry. Come on. They saved us seats," Madison says, almost dragging Brody to the opposite side of the barn. Once introductions are made, and everyone is seated, Madison goes to the restroom before the auction begins.

Bruce leans over to Brody and says, "are you THE Brody McGuire of BM Technologies?"

"Yes, but Madison doesn't know that," Brody replies.

"Why not?" Bruce demands.

Brody sighs. "Because I want her to like me for me, not my money."

"I can assure you Madison isn't like that. She doesn't need your money. I should know. Not only are we good friends, but I'm her financial advisor as well. Also, I look after her, so don't hurt her. Okay?"

"Look, Bruce. Madison and I are friends, nothing more. That's all we want from this relationship." Bruce nods. Nothing more is said because Madison has returned.

The auction begins with the livestock. Sitting beside Brody, Madison watches him out of the corner of her eye and enjoys the feeling of his shoulder touching hers. He is fascinated with the proceedings and doesn't notice Bruce left and returned with cold drinks for everyone. Brody leans over, occasionally asking questions about the auction; otherwise, he is in his own little world.

Once the livestock and poultry auction is over, the items from the women's building are up for bidding. Madison bids on several jams, cakes, and pies but never wins. However, when the clothing auction begins, Brody earnestly begins paying attention. He wants Madison to have the evening gown. Madison bids on two dresses and wins one, which makes Brody happy. He could tell she was getting a little downhearted at not winning any items.

Finally, the evening gown is up next. The starting bid is set for $500, which Madison bids. She has competition from several people. Brody watches with interest as the bidding continues at a feverish pace. Three bidders drop out when the bid reaches $1,000.

When the bid reaches $1,500, Brody notices Madison hesitate. He hears going once. She doesn't bid. Going twice. Madison still says nothing. Unable to control himself, Brody stands and yells $2,000. The auction barn grows silent.

"No, Brody," Madison says, reaching for his arm.

He looks down at her. "You will have that dress and wear it for me to the fundraiser next week." He gives her his most panty-dropping smile before looking up at the auctioneer.

"The bid is $2,000. Do I hear $2,100?" the auctioneer yells. Then, when no one responds, he yells, "going once, going twice. Sold to the gentleman in the blue shirt."

Brody beams with happiness. Madison shakes her head while Bruce and Perry laugh. "Now, what do I do?" Brody asks.

"Come on. I'll show you where to pay for that beautiful dress," Bruce punches Brody on the arm.

Chapter 20

MADISON

After they leave, Perry leans over to Madison. "I guess I know what you'll wear to the big event." She rolls her eyes and nods. "Let's go outside and wait for them. I'll text Bruce and let him know where we are."

"Perry, I can't believe he just did that."

"Why? A man wants his date to look beautiful, and you will definitely look stunning in that dress."

Madison looks at Perry with disdain. "I am not his date. We're just friends. Actually, we are still getting to know each other." Perry looks at her with a smirk and nods.

Perry and Madison are standing outside the main door to the auction barn when Bruce and Brody walk up. Bruce is wearing a big smile, while Brody looks like a little boy who got caught with his hand in the cookie jar.

"Brody, you didn't have to buy the dress," Madison says.

He smiles sheepishly and hands her a piece of paper. "Here's the girl's name and phone number. She'll expect your call on Monday so she can have the dress ready by Friday."

Madison takes the piece of paper. "Okay, you win. Now we need to make our way back to the parking lot. We don't want to miss the kickoff." Brody reaches for her hand, and they say their goodbyes to Bruce and Perry.

Walking through the fair back to the car, Brody stops in front of a game called high striker. "I want to see if I can do this," Brody says. He pays his fee and picks ups the massive hammer.

Madison stands behind him, watching, but she isn't watching the hammer or looking at the bell on top of the tower. Instead, she stares at the rippling muscles underneath Brody's T-shirt. Brody raises the hammer over his head, and the muscles of his biceps look like iron. As the hammer falls, the shirt's material is stretched across Brody's broad shoulders to the point Madison thinks the shirt might tear. I wonder what it would feel like to have those muscular arms around me, she ponders. The sound of the bell ringing interrupts her thoughts.

"Hey, Madison. I won," Brody yells. She joins in the clapping of the bystanders and smiles at him. Seconds later, he walks over to her carrying a giant stuffed squirrel. He hands it to her with a look of pride.

"A squirrel?" she says, laughing.

"It reminds me of the wildlife at the cabin," Brody answers, taking her hand.

The two talk about different attractions while walking back to the car. Madison can tell the day's excitement has been tiring for Brody, and her feet hurt from all the walking. When they reach the car, Brody places the stuffed squirrel in the back seat, sitting it upright to look like a passenger in the vehicle. He opens the door for Madison and then gets in. The drive home is silent at first. Madison looks over at Brody to see that he's dozed off. She smiles because her heart is full from making Brody feel young and free again.

"Brody. Brody," Madison says as she places her hand on his shoulder. "Brody, wake up. We're at the cabin."

"Oh, sorry. I must have dozed off. I didn't realize I was tired. I bet you are too."

"I'm good. Let's warm dinner, and then we'll watch the game." Madison opens her door, gets out of the SUV, and closes the door. When she turns around, Brody is right next to her.

"I really wish you would let me do that," he says, reaching for her hand.

The warmth of his hand radiates up her arm, and she pulls her hand away. "I don't think we'll get separated between here and the cabin." She walks toward the cabin with Brody following her.

After warming their dinner and eating, the pair spends the next three hours on opposite ends of the sofa watching the game. Finally, when the game ends, Madison yawns and carries her empty water bottle to the kitchen, as does Brody.

He walks up to her and places his hands on her shoulders. "Madison, thank you for a wonderful day. I can't remember when I've had so much fun." Brody leans in and kisses her lightly on the forehead. "This day has meant a lot to me."

"Your welcome, Brody. Thank you for the dress. What would you like to do tomorrow?"

"If you don't have any plans, I would like to take you out for brunch and the drive around the area. You can show me the sights."

"I don't have plans, and that sounds good. There aren't many sights to see, so we should be back in plenty of time for you to fish if you like. Good night, Brody. Sleep well." Madison turns and walks towards her bedroom. She feels Brody watching her but doesn't turn around.

In the shower, with the warm water running over her body, Madison thinks back to Brody with the hammer. She remembers the muscles in his back and arms. Madison relives the warmth of his touch on her hand and shoulders. Boy, I miss the touch of a man, she ponders. I wonder what it would be like to be touched all over by Brody. Oh well, she sighs. He is too young for me.

Stepping out of the shower, Madison wraps a towel around herself and hears the front door open. She stands by her door and listens. A few minutes later, the door opens again. Curious, Madison opens her door and walks out into the living area. Brody went out to the SUV and got the stuffed squirrel. He is placing it on the sofa facing the TV as if the squirrel is watching TV.

Unable to help herself, Madison laughs, startling Brody. He looks at her and smiles. Then she remembers she is wrapped in a towel. Madison hurries back into the bedroom and closes her door, smiling. She throws the towel into the bathroom, climbs into bed, and immediately falls asleep.

Chapter 21

MADISON

The aroma of coffee greets Madison when she opens her eyes. She looks at the clock, surprised to see it is 9:00 am. She hurries into the bathroom and then dresses in capris, a blouse, and sandals. Walking into the living area, Madison finds Brody sitting on the sofa, staring at his laptop.

"Good morning," she says.

Brody turns his head to look at her. "I hope you slept well. I slept like a rock," he says.

"I did. That coffee smells great. Do you need a refill?." Brody answers no, so Madison enters the kitchen and pours herself a cup. She returns and sits on the opposite side of the sofa from Brody. "You look serious," she remarks.

"I guess I do. I have a big meeting in the morning, and I was reading over the contract we will be discussing. That reminds me. I need to leave at 6:00 am. So I'll try not to wake you."

"No, I need you to wake me. I need to get up early. Before calling that girl about my dress fitting, I have things to do." Madison winks at Brody, and he smiles back.

"Madison, what time does the fundraiser start?"

"7:30. You're not canceling on me, are you?"

"No, but I'll be driving up on Saturday instead of Friday. I have meetings until late Friday and then on Saturday morning. I'll probably come straight from work."

Madison studies him for a minute and then says, "you work too much."

"I guess so. My assistant tells me that always, but that's what happens when you own your own business."

Brody has just given her some new information about himself, but she shows no surprise. "Don't you have a second in command that you could turn some of the work over to? If you don't, could you hire someone?"

"I do, and I probably could. Mike's been with me from the beginning."

"Do you trust him?" Madison asks.

"Yes, very much. He's a brilliant man and very trustworthy. You've given me something to think about," Brody says. "Now, are you ready for brunch?" Madison nods. "Good. I'm driving today."

Chapter 22

BRODY

After brunch, Brody and Madison drive over the entire county. She shows him the river and lake that he can fish at if he wants a change of scenery from the pond. Brody marvels at the beautiful countryside as he drives. Madison was right. There wasn't much to see, but having her with him is comfortable, and the conversation flows freely and easily.

On the way back to the cabin, Madison checks the TV schedule. They both agree they care nothing about the afternoon football matchups. So when they return to the cabin, Brody tells her he will change and go fishing. He gathers the fishing equipment and heads to the pond. After a short time, Madison walks up, carrying two folding chairs.

"If you don't mind the company, I thought I would enjoy the pleasant afternoon and read," she says.

"Only if you don't scare the fish away," Brody says with a smile, laying his fishing rod down and taking the chairs from her. He sets hers up where she wants and then takes his back to his fishing spot.

While he fishes, Brody's mind wanders back to what Madison said earlier about letting someone take over part of his work. He considered that a few years ago, but Mike wasn't ready, and Brody hated bringing in an outsider. On the other hand, maybe it was time to let Mike take over some workload. I'm not getting any younger, and I'm not ready to sell the company, but more free time would be great. I may talk to Angela this week and see what she thinks. At least I know I'll get an honest opinion from her. Brody snorts at the thought.

"Something funny?"

Brody turns at the sound of the voice. "Actually, yes. I was thinking about what you said earlier, and I may get my assistant's opinion on it."

"That's a little odd asking your assistant," Madison says.

"Angela, who you've talked to on the phone, is more than my assistant. She is a friend and confidant, a mother hen, and knows more about the business than I do. Sometimes, I wonder why I'm even there when she can do almost everything."

"Oh, okay. Good idea then," Madison says, glancing up from her laptop.

Brody lays his fishing rod down and walks over to Madison. "You've been very quiet." She looks into the dark blue and visibly trembles. "Are you cold, Madison?"

"No, I'm fine," she replies, looking down. "A prospective client has contacted me with an unusual personnel problem. I need to research the issue before deciding if I want to take on the job."

Brody sits on the ground facing her. "Why do the research? Why not just take the job?"

"Because Brody, I'm not like that. I take jobs where I believe I can make a difference or resolve an issue. I don't take jobs just for the money or the travel opportunities. If I think someone else could do a better job than me, I don't have a problem recommending them."

Thinking back to the background information Angela gave him about Madison, Brody isn't surprised by her answer. She has ethics, and he appreciates her honesty.

"Madison, where have you lived during your career?"

"Well, the bank I started work for sold or merged with another bank several times. I was fortunate to always have a job, even though I had to move after every sale or merger." Madison takes a breath. "I've lived in Seattle, Denver, Nashville, New York City, Houston, and Portland. I lived in Tampa, Phoenix, Los Angeles, and Baltimore for short periods. My favorite was Green Bay. I got to attend all the Packers' home games that year."

"Wow! I'm impressed," Brody says, looking at her in awe.

"And you thought I was just a small-town girl," Madison says, swatting his arm. "It's getting close to dinnertime. Why don't I go pick up some burgers?"

"I like that idea. Can I have onion rings with mine?" Brody asks like a small child, making Madison laugh.

"Of course. We can eat here or by the fire pit. Your choice."

"You go get the burgers. I'll put this stuff up and get a fire started. Oh, I'd like a strawberry milkshake, too," Brody says with a smile.

"Well, in that case, I'll have to hurry back so it won't melt," Madison replies, walking towards the cabin.

A few minutes later, Brody is carrying the last of the equipment to the cabin when he hears the SUV leave. This woman is so different from what I'm used to. She's more like Angela than any of the women I know. None of those women would go anywhere to pick up food, especially burgers.

Brody builds a fire and goes inside to pour himself a drink. He returns to the deck and watches the fire. His mind wanders back to Madison and how unusual she is. Maybe it's her maturity, but I doubt it. Years ago, I went out with a few women slightly older than me. They did not differ from the younger women. All they were interested in was money and status. He hears the SUV pull into the driveway and goes to help Madison with the food.

"That didn't take long," Brody states.

"Well, I called in the order to the convenience store where you bought your fishing bait."

"So are we eating beef, worm, or minnow burgers?" Brody teases as they walk to the deck.

Madison sits her bags on the table, places her hands on her hips, and says, "Brody McGuire, how dare you accuse me of feeding you bait? I'll have you know that place makes the best burgers in the county."

"Well, we'll see about that," he says, reaching into one bag and taking out his onion rings.

"Here's your milkshake."

"Where's yours?"

"I'm going to go get a bottle of water. Go ahead and get started. The burgers are identical." Madison walks into the cabin, but Brody waits for her.

When they finish eating, Brody says, "Madison, you were right. That was the best burger ever. The onion rings were perfect."

"What about the milkshake?" Madison asks with raised eyebrows.

"A few more strawberries would be nice." Brody winks, and Madison throws her napkin at him. "You sit, and I'll clean up this mess. Can I get you anything?"

"If you're going to have a drink, I'll take a glass of wine. There's an open bottle in the fridge." Brody gathers up the trash and carries it into the kitchen. Minutes later, he returns with his bourbon and Madison's wine. They sit quietly for a long time, enjoying the fire and the sunset.

"I better head to bed since we are getting up early in the morning." Madison states as she stands. "The fire is almost out, so everything's good out here. Please remember to wake me before you leave, Brody. Good night."

"Good night, Madison." Brody remains on the deck a little longer to finish his drink before heading inside to bed. Two whole days spent with Madison have been so relaxing. I may seriously consider giving Mikes some of my work.

Chapter 23

BRODY

Brody approaches Madison's bed quietly, so he doesn't startle her. He left the door open, and the light from the living area shines directly on her. He spends a few minutes observing her sleeping. Madison is lying facing him with her silver hair scattered over the pillow. But what catches Brody's attention most is her bare shoulders and back. The sheet is around her waist, and her arm covers most of her chest area. Brody inhales sharply. Oh wow, he says to himself. She sleeps naked.

The sight of Madison mesmerizes him. She looks so desirable lying there. Her skin looks like silk, inviting him to touch her. Brody reaches out but then quickly pulls his hand back. No, I can't be having thoughts like this if we are to be friends. But he continues to gaze at her for several seconds before remembering he needs to get on the road.

Brody carefully leans over, inhaling Madison's scent of lavender and vanilla. My gosh, she smells like heaven; he thinks. "Madison," he murmurs in her ear. "Madison, it's time to wake up."

She stirs, and it appears she will turn over on her back. Brody holds his breath, unable to look away. Instead, Madison opens her eyes and says, "okay. Give me a minute, and I'll be right there."

Minutes later, Madison walks out of her bedroom dressed in an oversized robe that hides her figure. Her hair is still a mess, but to Brody, she looks gorgeous. "Thanks for waking me. You be careful."

"I will do my best," he replies, walking to the door.

"Wait! You forget your leftovers." Madison rushes to the fridge, opens the door, and bends over.

Brody inhales deeply, looking at her behind. Then he walks toward her. "I don't want to forget those," he says. Madison hands him the bag of leftovers. "Okay. Well, goodbye. I'll be in touch." He quickly turns and leaves.

Three and a half hours later, Brody walks into his reception area. He places the bag of leftovers on Angela's desk. "Would you put this in the fridge for me? It's my lunch." He turns and walks toward his office, whistling. He opens the door and walks in, but before he can turn and close the door, Angela is there.

"What the heck, Brody?"

"What?"

"I've worked for you for twenty years. In all those years, you have never brought your lunch or whistled."

"I had a good weekend. That's all," he replies with his back to Angela as he walks toward his desk.

She rushes past him and sits in his chair. She points to the chair across from the desk. "Sit," Angela demands. Brody gives her a smirk and does as he's told. "Now, did you go to Pineville again?"

"Angela, you sure as nosy this morning."

"Answer me! Did you go to Pineville again?"

"Yes, as a matter of fact, I did. I had a fantastic weekend there. I had good luck fishing. Where's my coffee, by the way?"

Angela stares at Brody. "Coffee can wait. Did you see Ms. Donaldson again?"

"Yes."

"Brody, you're killing me here. Spill the beans."

"Oh, Angela. Is this how you treat your kids?" Brody asks with a smile.

"Yes, and I'm waiting for an answer. I can sit here all day if I need to." She leans back in Brody's chair, puts her feet on the corner of his desk, and crosses her arms.

"Okay. Okay. You win. Yes, I saw Madison."

"And?"

"She made dinner for me Friday night. Then she surprised me by taking me to the county fair the next day. We spent all day there. It was so much fun. Saturday night, we watched the Packers' game. Sunday, we went for a drive, and then I fished."

"And?"

"And she picked up burgers, and we ate beside the fire pit."

"Did she stay in the cabin with you?"

"Actually, she was having some work done at her house, so she slept in one bedroom, and I slept in the other. Nothing happened, Angela. Now, can we get to work?"

"Nope, not yet? Are you having feelings for this woman?" Angela asks with raised eyebrows.

Brody runs his fingers through his hair and looks at the floor. Then, when he looks up at Angela, he says, "not as you think. She's fun to be around. I feel so comfortable with her. Even when we don't talk, it's comforting to know she's there. She's just so different."

"Brody, look me in the eye and answer this question. What does she look like?"

"Well, she's about five foot seven with silver hair to her shoulders. She has a nice figure. She has the most beautiful green eyes I have ever seen. When she smiles, the entire world lights up."

"Hmmm."

"What does hmmm mean, Angela?"

"Nothing. I'm just thinking. Is that where your lunch came from?"

"Yeah. Madison is a superb cook. Her mac and cheese is the best I have ever eaten. I might give you a bite if you're nice to me at lunch."

"Ha! I'll be the one heating your lunch, so you can bet I'll taste it." Angela stands and strides to the door. "Mr. McGuire, you can have your desk back now. I have work to do, and your meeting starts in fifteen minutes. She closes the door behind her, but not before hearing the whistling again. Angela smiles, and says, "well, I'll be."

Chapter 24

BRODY

I t's not until noon on Wednesday that Brody can finally take a breath. Endless meetings, contract negotiations, and phone calls have taken up all his time. He's worked late in the evenings and gone to bed mentally and physically exhausted. Looking out his window, Brody realizes he hasn't messaged Madison so far this week. So he grabs his phone and types a quick message.

"Since I'm your plus one Saturday night, I need your address to pick you up."

Madison's response with her address is immediate.

"BTW—I have to leave Sunday. I have a flight to catch Monday morning," he sends. His jet is due for an annual maintenance check, so he has to fly commercially to Boston.

"That's okay. I fly out Monday morning too, so I'll have to leave early to drive to the Knoxville airport," Madison responds.

Brody rereads the message, and the wheels turn in his head. He looks out the window with the phone still in his hand. He looks up Madison's number and calls her.

"Hello, Brody!"

"Hi, Madison. I read your message and had an idea. What time is your flight Monday, and how long will you be gone?"

"Okay, I'm listening for your idea. My flight is at 10:00 am. I'll be back Thursday around 6:30," Madison replies.

"My flight is at 10:30," Brody says. "Why don't you come home with me on Sunday and spend the night? I have plenty of space, and you can see my apartment. Then I'll drive us to the airport on Monday morning and pick you up on Thursday."

"And bring me home on Friday?"

"Well, no," Brody hesitates. "I have a gala to attend on Saturday night. So I would very much like you to be my plus one."

"Can I think about it?" Madison asks.

"Of course. The gala is black tie, and besides, you owe me."

"Brody, why do I feel you're smiling?"

"Because I am, Madison. I always collect on my debts."

"Can I let you know later?"

"Sure. Have a good rest of the day. Goodbye." Brody hangs up the phone, very pleased with himself. It's time for Madison to see where and how he lives. Her being his plus one for the gala was a spur-of-the-moment thought and a good one. He can show off his new, beautiful friend to the gold diggers he usually takes to those mind-numbing events. "I hope she says yes to everything," he says aloud.

Chapter 25

MADISON

"Well, that was an interesting call," Madison says aloud when the phone line goes dead.

"What do you think?"

Madison shakes her head to clear her mind and looks at the girl standing before her. "What? I'm sorry. My mind was somewhere else."

"Probably on that handsome man that bought you this dress," the girl smiles broadly. "Are you pleased with how the dress fits?"

The girl moves to the side so Madison can look at herself in the full-length mirror. "I absolutely love it. You did a wonderful job." The girl hands Madison a mirror to look at the dress's back.

"I think you should get a pushup bra to show off your cleavage," the girl says. "But either way, you are going to be the envy of every woman at the fundraiser. I hope that handsome man appreciates how beautiful you look."

Madison blushes and starts removing the dress. "Thank you very much for the alterations. I guess I better get this to the cleaners and get it pressed."

"I'll press it for you. You can pick it up tomorrow. Tell Mr. McGuire thanks again for buying the dress. The money went directly into my scholarship fund."

"Would you be interested in earning money as a seamstress for me? I hate spending money on evening dresses that I only wear once or twice. I have four that could be reworked a little, so they look different."

"Oh, that would be fantastic. Since my project is finished, I have plenty of free time," the girl replies excitedly.

Madison continues removing the dress. "Great. Can I drop one off tomorrow when I pick up this dress?"

"Sure."

Madison hands the gown to the girl and says, "I'll call when I'm on my way. Thanks again."

Once in the car, Madison calls her stylist to verify her appointment for 3:00 Saturday to have her makeup and hair done at her home. Next, she makes an appointment for 9:00 Saturday morning for a mani-pedi. As she starts the SUV, Madison drives to Lexington to the mall. She needs new shoes to go with her dress, and she might as well invest in a new push-up bra.

On the drive back from Lexington, Madison considers Brody's proposal. He doesn't know that she plans to ask him to be her plus one in two weeks at another fundraising event. Staying at his place would save her from driving back and forth to Knoxville twice in one week.

When Madison arrives home, she goes to her closet, where she keeps her evening gowns. She selects an emerald one that she hasn't worn in two years. Uttering a silent prayer, it still fits when she tries it on. It fits perfectly. I can wear it to Brody's function. She checks her watch. Great. I have time to drop it off at the cleaners and pick it up on Friday. Madison changes back into her clothes and drops the gown off to be cleaned and pressed.

Climbing into bed, Madison grabs her phone and messages Brody, that she will take him up on his offer.

Chapter 26

MADISON

The stylist leaves Madison's house at 5:30. Madison stares at herself in the mirror, pleased with the makeup. The French twist hairstyle will leave her shoulders bare, but it is supposed to be a warm night. I'm as nervous as a girl on her first date. I still haven't heard from Brody. I hope he doesn't stand me up.

Madison goes to the fridge and pours a glass full of wine to calm her nerves. Then, she eats a few crackers because dinner won't be served until 8:30. God forbid, her stomach growls during the festivities.

Finally, at 6:00, her phone pings with a message from Brody. Unfortunately, he is stuck in traffic because of a wreck. He apologizes and asks if he can meet her at the event center because he doesn't want her to be late. Madison responds that's fine and sends him the address. Next, she texts Bruce and asks if he and Perry can pick her up. He replies yes, they will be there at 7:10.

Bruce, Perry, and Madison arrive at the event center at 7:20. Many guests have already arrived. Since she is an event co-chair, Madison leaves Bruce and Perry to make the rounds welcoming guests. Finally, back with Bruce and Perry, she checks her watch to see it is 8:00, and

90

Brody hasn't arrived yet. Madison turns her back to the door to speak to one guest.

Bruce leans over and whispers in Madison's ear, "your plus one has arrived." Madison notices Perry jab Bruce in the ribs before she turns around.

Standing at the door is the most handsome man Madison has ever seen. Dressed in a black tux that hugs his body, she can only lick her lips as she meets his eyes.

Chapter 27

BRODY

As usual, Brody feels out of place as he steps through the door of the event center. His eyes scan the room for Madison. Suddenly he spies her across the room, standing with her back to the door beside Bruce and Perry. She slowly turns around. His chest tightens as if all the air has been sucked out of his lungs.

Madison looks like a goddess in the black evening dress he bought her. She is wearing her hair up, so her creamy skin is visible. The dress dips in front to show off Madison's cleavage. The dress fits her body so well it could have been spray painted on. When her eyes meet his, and she licks her lips, Brody almost melts into a puddle on the floor.

She smiles, and her eyes light up. At that moment, there is no one else in the room but the two of them. Brody watches her mouth move, and then she walks toward him. No, she's floating toward him. All Brody can do is stand there and stare at the beautiful woman coming his way.

When Madison finally reaches him, she rises on her tiptoes, placing her hands on his shoulders. "Hi, Brody," her warm breath brushes his ear as she kisses him softly on the cheek.

"Wow! Madison. You take my breath away," he says honestly. "You look stunning."

"Thank you, Brody. You look good enough to eat yourself," she replies shyly.

"Shall we?" Brody asks, offering her his arm. Madison takes it, and Brody is swept into a whirlwind of introductions and small talk. Madison briefly leaves him with Bruce and Perry to check on dinner and quickly returns. The master of ceremonies asks everyone to take their seats so dinner may be served.

Madison leads Brody to one of the head tables, where they sit and enjoy a delicious dinner and small talk. After dinner, the president of the county humane society gives a speech. When he's finished, a band plays in the background.

"I believe I owe you a dance," Brody whispers in Madison's ear. She nods, smiles, and stands. He moves her to the dance floor and takes her into his arms. For Brody, no one else exists on the dance floor but him and Madison. She is an excellent dancer and feels so right in his arms. They don't talk but enjoy the music.

As the pair glides across the floor, Brody thinks back to other events he had attended in the past. He hated dancing, or was it the women he was dancing with that he hated? Dancing with Madison is like being in a dream. Then, suddenly, he feels a tap on his shoulder. Brody turns his head and stops dancing.

"Brody, old man. Where have you been hiding this gorgeous woman?" the man asks.

"Ted, what are you doing here?"

"Contributing to a worthy cause. Aren't you going to introduce us?"

"Madison, this is my friend from Knoxville, Ted Mathis. Ted, this is Madison Donaldson."

"Hi, Madison. Can I cut in?" Ted doesn't wait for Brody to answer. Instead, he pushes him out of the way and grabs Madison. Brody moves to the edge of the dance floor and watches closely. He smelled the liquor on Ted's breath, which sometimes means trouble. Brody sees Ted talking to Madison. She only nods or shakes her head. She looks very uncomfortable, so Brody heads back to Madison when the dance ends.

"Ted, I would like my date back now," Brody says gruffly.

"Of course, Brody. Not only is Madison a beauty, but she's an excellent dancer." Ted backs away, and Brody takes Madison in his arms, holding her against him for a slow dance.

"Are you okay?" Brody whispers against Madison's neck.

"Yes, but my gut tells me to be wary of him," she whispers back.

Brody lifts his head and looks into her eyes. "He's a friend, but trust your instincts," he whispers. Madison nods and places her head on his shoulder.

After two more dances with Madison, Brody is forced to give her up to dance with Bruce and then Perry. After that, the four sit and talk. Too soon, the announcement is made that it's time for the last dance of the night. Brody stands and offers his hand to Madison. She takes it, and he leads her to the dance floor.

Brody pulls her against him and holds her tightly. I wish this night would never end; he thinks. It has been a perfect night with my beautiful lady beside me.

While Brody and Madison wait for the valet to deliver Brody's car, he holds her hand, squeezing it slightly. She doesn't pull her hand away this time. Finally, a very expensive car pulls up, and Brody opens the door. Madison looks at him, confused. Brody smiles and says, "you didn't really think I would pick you up in the pickup, did you?" Madison giggles and gets into the car.

Madison invites Brody in when they reach her house. He's excited to see her home and admires the living area. The place is well-decorated and feels comfortable.

"Brody, would you like a drink?"

"Yes, please. The house is beautiful, Madison."

"Thank you." She hands him his drink and pours a glass of wine for herself. "Brody, it's almost midnight. Why don't you stay here tonight instead of driving to the cabin? I have a spare bedroom with a private bathroom."

"That's very kind of you to offer. It's been a long week, and I'm pretty tired. I'll take you up on your offer if you don't mind. Let me get my stuff out of the car." Brody sets his glass down and walks outside. Moments later, he's back with an overnight bag.

Madison shows him to the bedroom. Brody tosses his bag on the bed. "Madison, I had a wonderful time. I have never enjoyed a fundraiser as much as I did tonight."

"I'm so glad, Brody. That means a great deal to me." She pauses and looks him in the eye. "You're a very handsome man, Brody. Any woman would be proud to have you by her side."

"Madison, you are more stunning in that dress than I imagined you would be."

"Thank you so will you unzip me so I can go to bed?" She turns her back to Brody.

Brody slowly walks behind her, admiring the view. Man, I would love to kiss those shoulders and help her out of that dress, he thinks. But Brody keeps his thoughts to himself and unzips the dress, gazing at her creamy skin as the teeth of the zipper part. Then, finally, he takes a deep breath and says, "all done" when he's finished.

"Goodnight, Brody. Sleep well," Madison says, walking out the door and closing it behind her.

"Sleep well?" Brody whispers. "Maybe after I take a cold shower, I can."

Chapter 28

MADISON

Madison tossed and turned all night. She couldn't get the vision of the handsome man in the tux out of her mind. Nor could she forget the way their eyes locked when she first saw him in the doorway. Or how his finger brushed her back as he unzipped her dress, causing an unfamiliar warm rush of feelings down her body. Get a grip, Madison tells herself. This is a friendship, not a relationship.

Wearing jeans and a polo, Madison walks into her kitchen to find Brody sitting at the table, drinking coffee and looking at his laptop. "Good morning," he says, smiling.

"Good morning to you," she returns the smile. "How did you sleep?"

"I did fine, and you?"

"I slept okay," Madison lies.

"The game comes on at three. Would it be okay if we went out for brunch, and then we head to my place?" Brody asks.

"Sounds good. I'm looking forward to seeing your home."

"Don't expect much because it's a bachelor pad, after all."

"It's your home, Brody."

"Most of the time, it doesn't feel like home," he replies wistfully.

Madison doesn't comment but pours a cup of coffee and refills his cup. She sits down across from him and asks, "are you working again?"

"Yes, I'm just reading over a contract for tomorrow. Are you ready to go?" Madison nods and heads to her bedroom.

After loading the car and brunch, Brody concentrates on driving because it has begun to rain. The car is too quiet for Madison.

"Brody, tell me about the event Saturday night."

"Well, my dear, you aren't the only animal lover. It is for the zoo and I'm on the board. Even though it is black tie, the gala is being held at the zoo."

"That sounds interesting and fun."

"It will be different since it is usually held at the convention center. The planning committee decided if people tire of dancing, talking, and drinking, they can walk through the zoo and view the animals."

"I'm looking forward to it," Madison says.

"Me too, especially since you'll be my date." Brody reaches over and pats her on the knee. "Now, where are you flying to tomorrow, and is it business or pleasure?"

"I'm going to Baltimore, and it's both. I am trying to help a friend whose business is in trouble."

"May I ask what kind of work you'll be doing?"

Madison tells Brody her friend, Brad, owns a technology company specializing in game applications. Brad owns twenty-five of the top one hundred games people play on their smart devices. He employs fifty people, but between salary expenses and medical insurance, he may have to lay off employees for the business to survive. Madison says her friend has cut overhead as much as possible and sees no other way. Her friend has been upfront with the employees, and her job will be to help develop a severance package.

"Wow, that's tough. I would have thought he would roll in money owning that many games," Brody says.

"You would think so, but he pays his employees very well. I have played none of his games, but I have looked at them. The graphics are amazing."

"Has he considered selling the company in order to save it?"

Madison considers for a few seconds before answering. "If I recall, he said he's had a couple of offers from foreign companies, but he wants to keep it American-owned. He's a military veteran, and that's very important to him."

The rest of the drive is quiet until Brody pulls up to a high-rise apartment building in downtown Knoxville. A gentleman meets the car at the curb and opens the door for Madison, greeting her as Ms. Donaldson.

Brody exits the car and walks around to stand beside Madison. "Hi, George," he says as he tosses the car keys in the man's direction. "

The man nods and smiles. "Welcome home, Mr. McGuire. Joyce is waiting for you."

Brody offers his arm to Madison and says, "let's go."

"What about my bags?" Madison asks.

"George will bring them up to the apartment," Brody answers.

Madison takes in the vast expanse of the building's lobby. Decorated in creams and browns, the entrance has several seemingly expensive paintings adorning the walls. Brody guides her to the elevator. When the door opens, he punches in a code, and the elevator rises. Madison remains quiet during the ride to the apartment.

When the elevator door opens, Brody extends his arm for Madison to walk in first. She steps into a foyer where a woman about her age is waiting. "Madison, this is Joyce. She runs the household. Joyce, this is Madison Donaldson, our guest for the evening." Madison shakes Joyce's offered hand, then Joyce turns and walks out of sight.

"Come on," Brody says. "I'll show you to your room and then give you a tour of the place."

"Brody, this place is enormous. Do you live here alone?" Madison asks.

"No, Joyce and George live here too. They have their own suite." Brody takes her hand and leads Madison upstairs and into the first door on the left." This is your room any time you want to stay here."

The room is massive, but the windows draw Madison in. They are floor-to-ceiling and look out over the city of Knoxville. "Wow, Brody. This view is gorgeous," she says, walking to the windows.

Chapter 29

BRODY

Not as gorgeous as what I'm looking at, Brody thinks, staring at Madison from behind. The sun has broken through the clouds and is shining directly on Madison, making her glow. "It is a marvelous view," he says, standing next to her. "George will bring everything up shortly. If you think of anything you need, please let Joyce or me know. Now, are you ready for the tour?" he asks proudly. Madison nods and Brody offers her his hand, which she takes.

Brody shows her three additional bedrooms upstairs that are smaller than Madison's. Next, the pair heads downstairs, where Brody gives her a tour of the library/TV room, the kitchen and dining area, and the living area. All the rooms have the floor to ceiling windows with the same view as Madison's bedroom.

Next, Brody takes her to a long hallway. On the right are his office and bedroom. Letting go of her hand, he walks to a closed door across from his office. "This is my playroom," he says. Madison takes a sharp breath with visions of playrooms that look like torture chambers she has seen in movies.

Brody chuckles as if he has read her mind and opens the door. "This is my game room. I have an X-box, pool and foosball tables, and this," he points to a table on the right. "This is where we play poker when it's my night to host. By the way, Ted texted me and said he had to move the game here Thursday because he's having some remodeling done at his place. I will have plenty of time to pick you up at the airport, though."

"I thought I got a whiff of cigars," Madison adds with a smile.

"Yeah, I hate cigars, but some guys smoke them while we play. I'm surprised you can smell it because I have a separate ventilation system in here just for that reason. Down at the end of the hallway are Joyce and George's quarters. They are married and have been with me about fifteen years." Brody looks at Madison almost apologetically." What do you think of the place?"

Madison grabs his hand and looks up at him. "I think it's fantastic and I have to know if you decorated it?"

Pleased with her reaction, Brody says, "no, my mother did. She and her husband live downstairs when they're in town. Oh, look, it's almost time for the game. Joyce made snacks for us to munch on." He leads her back to the kitchen, where Joyce has made a feast of different snacks. "You start, and I'll go turn the TV on."

Brody goes into the TV room and quickly surveys the furniture. I want to sit close to Madison, but I don't want her to be uncomfortable. So first, he grabs several pillows off the sofa and tosses them into two empty chairs. Next, he places a Packers logo throw onto the back of the couch and moves several items around on the coffee table to make room for their plates. Last, he turns on the TV.

Madison walks into the room with food and drink as Brody turns around. He watches as she places her glass and plate on the coffee table. Then, she sits on the floor, leaning back against the sofa. Okay, I can live with that, he thinks.

After getting his food and drink and placing them on the coffee table, he returns to the kitchen and grabs a plate of cookies. He sets those on the coffee table in front of Madison, who grins at him. Finally, Brody sits on the couch so his leg is a mere inch from her arm.

Brody leans over to retrieve his plate and gets a whiff of Madison's lavender and vanilla shampoo. He inhales deeply, as if committing the fragrance to memory. Her silver hair looks so silky and shiny that he is tempted to run his fingers through it. Then, I would move her hair to the side and kiss her neck and the hollow under her cute ear.

"Brody, did you see that?" Madison yells.

It takes a minute for her question to register in Brody's mind. "What?"

"The Packers kicked off and fumbled the ball." She looks over her shoulder at him. "Are you watching the game?"

"Sure, I am," Brody replies with a grin. I'm watching all right, but not the game. I need to quit daydreaming.

When Madison finishes eating, she yawns and moves to sit on the end of the sofa. "You're sleepy," Brody says, and she nods. He stands, retrieves a pillow from a chair, and sits down, placing the pillow on his lap. "Lay down here and take a nap," he says, patting the cushion. "I don't mind."

Madison lays her head on the pillow in Brody's lap. He reaches for the throw and covers her. In minutes, Madison's softly breathing and Brody watches her sleep. She looks like an angel, he thinks.

When Madison turns on her side to face him, Brody eases a lock of hair from her face. His knuckles lightly brush her soft cheek. She stirs and turns onto her back. Now, he has a chance to really study her face without makeup. Even without makeup, Madison is a beautiful woman. She has a few tiny wrinkles at the corners of her eyes, but her lashes are long and naturally dark. Her lips are full and a dark shade of pink. Brody feels his body react to Madison strongly.

When Brody can't take it any longer, he runs his hands over her silky hair. Madison stirs and opens her eyes, looking directly into his. The emerald eyes are captivating, pulling Brody under her spell. He wants to kiss her so badly.

As if sensing Brody's feelings, Madison smiles and sits up. "How's the game going?" she asks.

"I, uh, I don't know," he stammers. "I guess I dozed off, too," he lies and looks up at the TV. The game is over. Gosh, I guess I watched her sleep for two hours. Madison reaches to remove the pillow from his lap, but Brody keeps his hand on it. He has to because of his body's reaction to her.

Madison pulls her hand back and says, "it looks like the game is over. So I'm going to get my laptop and work a little while."

Once she heads up the stairs, Brody removes the pillow and looks down. "I need to go to my bathroom and take care of you," he whispers to his lap.

When Brody returns, Madison is sitting on the sofa with her feet tucked under her studying her laptop. She looks up at him. "Brody, are you okay because your face is flushed?"

"Yeah, I'm fine," he replies, turning a bright red shade. "Are you hungry? I can see what Joyce left for dinner." Madison would never return if she knew what I was doing.

"I am a little hungry, so I'll go with you."

The pair finds chicken Caesar salad in the fridge and a loaf of French bread on the counter. While Madison serves the salad, Brody slices the bread and selects a bottle of wine.

Later, while they clean the kitchen, Brody says, "I need to go over that contract again. Do you need to work more?" Madison nods. "Do you want to come to my office or stay in the TV room?"

"I think the TV room because it's comfy in there."

"Mind if I join you?" Brody says. Madison shakes her head. "Okay, I'll be there shortly. I need to email Mike at the office first."

Brody opens his laptop in his office and emails Mike, with Urgent on the subject line. "Find out about a game application company in Baltimore owned by a man named Brad. They are in a financial bind. I heard they own twenty-five of the top games and have outstanding graphics. We need that if we are going to get into the gaming business. Email me with the info as soon as you have it." After the email is sent, Brody joins Madison in the TV room, where they work silently until bedtime.

Brody is about to change clothes when there's a knock at his door. "Come in," he says with his back to the door.

"Uh, Brody." He turns to find Madison in his doorway, wrapped in a towel. "I forgot to pack a gown, so could I borrow a T-shirt?"

He bites the inside of his cheek as he looks at her. I would love to rip that towel off her right this minute. But he lowers his eyes, turns, and walks to his dresser. He pulls out a T-shirt and tosses it to Madison.

Brody hears her say thanks and watches the door close behind her. "Well, back to the bathroom," he says aloud, looking below his waist.

Chapter 30

MADISON

Madison listens at the closed door and doesn't hear a sound. That's a good sign that no one is up yet, she determines. She quietly opens the door and stands at the top of the stairs, listening again. Finally, satisfied all is quiet, Madison pads downstairs in her bare feet to the coffee pot.

The coffee pot is almost finished when she hears, "did you make enough for two?" Madison jumps. "Sorry. Did I scare you?" She nods as Brody walks around the island toward her. He eyes her up and down. "That T-shirt never looked that good on me," he remarks with a huge grin.

Madison looks down at the T-shirt and blushes. "I'm sorry, but I forgot my robe, too." Oh, brother, she thinks. Here I stand with nothing on but this T-shirt, and it is white. I should have asked for a colored one.

"I didn't mean to embarrass you, Madison, but you look relaxed, making me hope you feel at home here."

"I do," she replies, pouring coffee for both of them. "Now, if you'll excuse me, I better get dressed." Madison can feel Brody's eyes following her, and I have to walk right past the sunlight-filled windows in this flimsy white T-shirt, she whispers low?

Later, showered and fully dressed, Madison steps into the kitchen to find Brody dressed in a white button-down shirt and gray slacks. "Well, don't you look like a professional business executive about to board an airplane to parts unknown?" Madison comments. Brody smiles at her, but Joyce lets out a little giggle from the cooktop.

"I'll have you know, young lady, I'm off to Portland this morning. And speaking of looking professional, look at you. I haven't seen you in a suit before."

Madison pirouettes in front of him, showing off her black suit with a dark green blouse. "I try not to make a habit of dressing like this when I fly, but I won't have time to change before my meeting." She looks into Brody's eyes and watches as they darken before he glances away.

"Ms. Donaldson, what can I make for you for breakfast?" Joyce asks.

"I'll just have toast, thank you," Madison replies. "What are you having, Brody?"

"I already ate. We'll need to leave for the airport soon, so I'll get my bag. Madison, are your bags ready?"

"Yes, they're by the door, thanks."

Brody leaves the room as Joyce places the toast in front of Madison. "Ms. Donaldson, Mr. McGuire said you will return on Thursday and stay until Sunday. Is there anything I can do for you or get for you while you're gone?"

"Please call me Madison, and yes, I need something. I need a stylist to do my hair and makeup on Saturday afternoon."

Joyce nods. "I can take care of that for you. What time would work for you?"

"I didn't ask Brody when the gala started, but four hours before that will work."

"Great. I'll talk to Mr. McGuire, find out when he plans to leave, and make the appointment accordingly."

"Thanks, Joyce. Here comes Brody. I better grab my bag."

A big black SUV pulls up to the curb where Madison and Brody wait. He opens and closes the back door for her, then goes around and gets in. George is in front driving. Madison leans over. "Brody, which vehicle is your favorite?" she asks with a smile.

He grins back and answers, "the pickup, of course."

The ride to the airport is short and quiet. Once they pull up to the curb, Madison starts to open her door, but Brody grabs her arm and gives her a look. She giggles and sits back while he gets out. When he opens her door, he says, "now you get the idea."

George sets the bags on the curb and tells them goodbye. Madison reaches for her suitcase, but Brody gives her another look. This time, she rolls her eyes at him.

"Madison, are you checking your bag?" She nods. Brody grabs his carry-on and rolls it and her suitcase into the terminal.

She follows him, watching him walk through the terminal. Brody is confident and comfortable in his own skin. Women look at him appreciatively; some even lick their bright red painted lips as he passes, but he ignores them.

Madison observes Brody's crisp, white fitted shirt hug his broad shoulders and arms. She follows the shirt down to his tapered waist. Then on to his cute behind in those fitted gray slacks. The slacks appear to caress his muscular legs as he walks. Suddenly, Madison feels a warmth spreading through her body to her core. Desire courses through her veins like a wildfire in a dry forest. She stops and closes her eyes, relishing feelings she thought she had lost years ago.

"Madison, are you okay?" She opens her eyes to find Brody staring at her. Embarrassed, she quickly nods her head. "Are you sure because you look feverish?"

"I, I, I'm okay, Brody. You are walking too fast for me in these heels." She watches him look down at her five-inch heels.

Brody, suitcases and all, walks up to her. He stands only a few inches from her. Then, he leans down and whispers in her ear, "there's a time and place for sexy heels like that. Airports are not one of those places."

When Brody's hot breath hits her ear, everything below Madison's waist grows wet. Unable to help herself, she looks into his eyes and watches as they turn dark. Brody looks down at her lips, and she runs her tongue over her top lip. Madison feels the tension between them growing by the instant. This isn't how it's supposed to be, she decides and steps back, still watching him.

Brody lets go of her suitcase, and it falls to the floor with a thud. He looks down and runs his fingers over his chin while Madison watches, wishing it were her fingers. Then, finally, he takes a heavy breath and says, "Madison, I'm sorry."

She stands still until his eyes meet hers. "I'm not," she says and walks off toward the checked baggage line, leaving Brody to follow her.

Brody waits for Madison as she checks her bag, and they go through security together. Brody's gate is two away from hers, so they sit together silently, drinking coffee. Then, when it's Madison's time to board, they both stand.

Madison looks up at Brody. He reaches up and lightly touches her cheek. "Good luck, princess. I'll see you when you return." She kisses him tenderly on the cheek and wishes him luck as well. He turns and begins walking toward his gate.

Madison watches Brody walk away and then boards the plane. She contemplates their exchange at the airport the entire flight to Baltimore. I really like him as a friend, but I may be falling too deep into something I didn't want. I do not know how he feels. He rarely lets his feelings show, and when they do, he hides them quickly. Maybe we're spending too much time together. At least I have a few days to think about it without him around.

Chapter 31

BRODY

By the time Brody grabs a bourbon and reaches his gate, it's time for him to board the plane. He gulps the bourbon and walks onto the plane, ordering another bourbon as he passes the flight attendant in first class. After the attendant brings him the bourbon, Brody lays his seat back.

What the heck happened in the airport? he asks himself. One minute we were walking to the counter to check Madison's suitcase, and the next, we had a moment of primal desire. Madison felt it, too. I know she did. I couldn't help myself. She looked so dang sexy in those heels, and I almost melted when she ran her tongue over her top lip. I wonder if she did that to tease me or if she desires me as much as I do her.

Brody's phone pings with an email. He quickly opens his laptop and pulls up the email, saving it before putting the phone and laptop on airplane mode. Please, please let it be something to take my mind off Madison, he pleads silently.

After the plane takes off, Brody opens the email. It's from Mike. The email says the company Brody was inquiring about was easy to find. Unfortunately, the owner, Brad Wilkerson, is deep in debt to the

109

tune of \$2.5M. Mike talked to several of Brody's employees, who said Brad was one of the best developers in the world. Unfortunately, Brad hadn't been able to work in that area because he was trying to keep his business afloat. Salary expenses and medical insurance costs were eating him alive, and word of the street was bankruptcy.

Mike's email also says Brody's employees say the games' graphics are by far the best they have ever seen. If Brody's interested in getting into the game business, this may be the company to go after. Then he can forget the possible partnership with the overseas company Brody has been talking to.

Brody closes his eyes. He has been considering getting into games, but the overseas company demanded more money than he wanted to pay. Also, he preferred to stick with American companies but hadn't found one suitable.

This buyout may be the perfect opportunity to see what Mike can handle. Brody drafts an email to Mike telling him to come up with a proposal they can discuss when he returns to the office on Wednesday. He'll email when the plane lands.

Yawning, Brody closes his eyes and quickly falls asleep. He dreams of a beautiful silver-haired woman dressed only in his white T-shirt and wearing sexy heels walking toward him. He wakes with a jump and reaches for a nearby blanket to cover his lap before the flight attendant walks by.

Chapter 32

BRODY

Brody waits inside the terminal by baggage claim for Madison. Thankfully, he's been too busy to give her much thought since his plane ride to Portland. Mike developed an outstanding proposal for the owner of the gaming company, which is also Madison's friend and client. Brody informed Mike that he is to take the lead on the proposal, so Mike will fly to Baltimore next week to talk to Brad Wilkerson.

He feels her before he sees her. Brody looks at the escalator and sees Madison dressed in jeans and a polo shirt. She looks tired, he thinks. That's not good. When she spots Brody in the crowd, Madison smiles broadly, lighting up the entire baggage claim area and Brody's world. He matches her smile with his own and hurries to meet her.

"Hi. Welcome back, Madison."

"Hi, yourself, and thanks for meeting me. I'm sorry the plane was delayed."

"No problem whatsoever. Let's grab your bag and get back to my place because you look tired," Brody says, placing his hand across her lower back to guide her to the correct carousel.

Once inside the pickup, Brody asks about her trip. Madison says it was long and talking to her client was very depressing. In addition, two of her friends had to cancel dinner because of illness.

"I'm sorry. I was hoping you had a pleasant trip. Now I have bad news. I was hoping to have a quiet dinner with you before the poker game, but since your flight was delayed, I won't be able to. The guys are already arriving at the apartment."

"That's okay," Madison says. "I'll just grab something to eat later and stay in my room."

"Joyce always makes sandwiches and snacks for the game. So there'll be plenty to eat. Would you like me to fix you a plate?"

"Thanks, but I'm not hungry right now."

When they reach the apartment, Brody carries Madison's suitcase up to her room. Madison follows him and lies down on the bed. "I may take a little nap."

"Okay. I'll have my phone, so text me if you need anything."

"Thank you for everything, Brody." He quietly leaves the room and closes the door. I hope she's okay and not coming down with something, he mutters.

"Well, the loser has finally arrived," Ted announces as Brody walks into his game room. Everyone is seated at the table and stands to shake his hand.

"You guys ready to give all your money away?" Brody grins as he takes his seat at the table.

The men have played poker for two hours when Ted announces all the sandwiches are gone. Brody tells him more are in the fridge, so Ted leaves to get them. He returns a few minutes later, dragging Madison behind him.

"Look who I found in the kitchen," Ted announces. All the men stand but Brody. He has his back to the door and looks over his shoulder. "This is Brody's friend, Madison. Madison, this is Tom, Jackson, Bradley and Ben." All the men shake hands with Madison except Ben.

"Ben and I already know each other," Madison says. "Gentlemen, it's very nice to meet each of you. I'm sorry to interrupt, but Ted insisted. So I'll leave now and say good night."

As she turns to leave, Ben says, "Madison, may I have a word with you?" and follows her out.

"Ted, you forgot the sandwiches," Brody says. "I'll go get them." Brody quietly heads to the kitchen and sees Ben and Madison standing by the windows.

"What do you want, Ben?" Madison asks.

"Oh, come on, Madison, sweetheart. You know exactly what I want. We had some good times together," he chuckles.

"You might have had a good time, but I didn't, and it was only twice. Besides, you're married now, I understand, and I don't go out with married men."

"Madison, you would have had a good time if you had just relaxed."

"Ben, I don't consider being handcuffed and beaten with a whip a good time. Your kinky idea of sex makes me sick."

"The sex was good, though, even if it was in the dark," Ben says.

"No, Ben, the sex wasn't that good. Now, leave me alone and go back to your game," Madison says, walking away.

Brody ducks behind the kitchen island when Ben walks past so he's not seen. Then he quickly stands, grabs the sandwiches, and hurries back to the game.

As Brody walks into the room, he overhears Ted saying, "I didn't know you knew Madison, Ben."

"It was many years and three wives ago. But she's still a beautiful woman," Ben remarks.

"How was she in the sack?" Ted asks, grinning like a fool.

Brody feels his stomach churning and says, "Ted, that's none of your business."

"Maybe you already know the answer, Brody. You should tell your buddy Ted all about it."

"Ted, you've had too much to drink. Why don't you go home?"

As the other men around the table look from Brody to Ted and back, Brody quietly says, "Madison and I are friends, that's all?"

"Friends with benefits, I bet."

"Ted, that's enough," Ben says, harshly. "Madison is a lady, and I won't stand for you to talk about her like one of your common whores."

"All right, all right. I was just trying to have a little fun. So let's get back to playing cards," Ted says.

After the comments about Madison, Brody can no longer concentrate on the game and loses every hand. After everyone leaves, he cleans up their mess. Brody hates for Joyce to deal with the cigars, spilled food and drinks, and leftover food. He's carrying empty beer bottles into the kitchen when he encounters Madison at the fridge.

"Madison, I didn't see you there," Brody says, surprised. "Can I get you something?"

"I couldn't sleep, so I thought maybe a glass of wine might help me relax."

"Let me set this down, and I'll get you a glass. I think I need to find a bottle and open it."

"Please don't go to any trouble this late, Brody. I can just drink water or juice."

Brody walks past her to the wine cooler. "It's no trouble. Can I join you, or would you prefer to be alone?"

"I'd enjoy your company, but don't you have to go to bed so you can go to work in the morning?"

As he opens the bottle of wine, Brody tells her, "I never know how late the poker game will run, so I rarely go in until after lunch or not at all. It depends on what's going on at the office." He pours her a glass of wine and himself two fingers of bourbon. They sit side by side at the island.

"I'm sorry I barged into your game, but Ted found me in the kitchen. He grabbed my arm and dragged me in there. I know he's your friend, but I don't enjoy being around him."

"That's okay, I understand. Ted has changed a lot in the last couple of years. He got involved with a BDSM group that Ben's involved with. Ted has a short attention span. I thought he'd grow tired of that group by now, but he seems to get deeper and deeper into it," Brody says, staring at his glass.

Madison touches his arm. "What about you, Brody? Are you into that sort of thing?"

Brody lays his free hand on hers and looks into her eyes. "No, Madison. I respect women too much, and the idea of physically hurting someone makes me sick." The conversation he heard between Madison and Ben replays in his mind. "What about you, Madison? Are you into that kind of stuff?"

"Oh gosh, no! That stuff scares me, and I hate pain as much as heights."

With his hand still on hers, Brody says, "Madison, tell me your idea of your ideal man."

She laughs. "You better pour us another drink for this deep discussion because I want to hear about your ideal woman afterward." He reaches for the bottles and refills their glasses.

"Let's see," Madison begins. "My ideal man would be thoughtful, kind, compassionate, honest, and generous. I'm not talking money. I'm talking about his time, attention and willingness to share his feelings. Someone to make love with and is unselfish in his lovemaking. A man that listens to my breathing, gasps, and moans to learn what satisfies me. A man that makes me melt with only a look or a touch. That's all that comes to me off the top of my head. Now, your turn."

"My perfect partner would have most of the same traits you just described. But, she would also be one that when I look across the room at her, her eyes would say I'm yours and only yours now and forever."

"Have you ever met your ideal woman, Brody?"

Brody takes a deep breath and holds it for a few seconds. "Honestly, no. Looking back, I think I wanted so badly for one of my fiancée's to be the perfect woman, that I overlooked the obvious signs that they weren't. There is one woman that has come very close, though. I'm still learning about her. What about you? Have you ever met your idea of the perfect man?"

Madison looks at her glass and contemplates her answer. "I have met men with a few of the traits but never the complete package. But, like you, I have met a man looking more and more like the man I would like to spend the rest of my life with, but..." Her voice drifts off.

"But what, Madison?"

"But he's younger than I am so I have to consider that. I'm very old to fall in love and be hurt again."

"A person is never too old to fall in love, Madison," Brody says softly. "Now, it's almost 2:00 am and we should probably go to bed."

"Yeah, you're right. Sorry I kept you up so late."

"Are you wearing another one of my T-shirts?" Brody looks her up and down as she slides off the stool.

Madison giggles and puts her hands on her hips. "Yeah. You were busy, and I couldn't find Joyce, so I helped myself to one of your shirts. They are very comfortable to sleep in." She punches him lightly on the arm.

"I know they are. Well, you can help yourself to anything in my room."

"I already did," Madison says, walking away giggling like a little girl.

I wonder what that means; Brody thinks as he walks to his room yawning. That second glass of bourbon made me more sleepy than I already was. I'll shower in the morning after I text Angela that I'm taking the entire day off.

Chapter 33

MADISON

The following morning, Madison is up early. She tiptoes to the end of the hallway, peering down at the kitchen. She doesn't see Brody, but she sees Joyce. Madison catches Joyce's eye and motions her over to the stairs.

"Good morning, Madison."

"Hi, Joyce. Where's Brody?"

"He's in his office. I was making his breakfast."

Madison grins. "I want to have a little fun with him. Would you mind playing along?" Joyce nods with a smile and quickly returns to the kitchen. Madison retreats to her room to wait until Brody is seated at the island.

Fifteen minutes later, Madison opens her door quietly. She can hear Brody and Joyce talking while Brody holds the newspaper in front of him. Madison bounces down the stairs. "Good morning", she says in a chipper voice—both Joyce and Brody answer.

Brody peers over his newspaper at Madison and says, "are those my socks?"

"Yeah, but they're too big for me," Madison answers, bending over to pull the socks up with her behind pointing to Brody. Joyce giggles quietly and turns her back to the pair.

"Are those my boxers, too?" Brody asks in a deep voice.

"What can I say? I ran out of underwear and needed something to wear," Madison replies, shrugging her shoulders.

"Good gosh, woman. Joyce, please do Madison's laundry. I'm not in the mood or have time to buy more boxers, T-shirts, and socks today." Brody lifts the newspaper as if to block the view of Madison.

"Yes, sir. I'll get right on it," Joyce replies with a smirk.

"Brody, do you have plans for us today?" Madison asks innocently.

Brody doesn't move the newspaper but says, "yes and we should leave in thirty minutes."

"I won't have Madison's laundry finished by then," Joyce states.

Madison turns to walk to the stairs and waits for Brody to take a sip of coffee. "That's okay, Joyce. I'll just go commando." Brody spits coffee all over his newspaper. Both women giggle. "Come on, Joyce. I'll get my laundry for you," Madison says. Joyce follows Madison up the steps, still laughing.

"I know you're talking about me," the deep voice says, and the two women laugh all over again.

Joyce follows Madison into the bedroom. "Madison, that was so funny."

"Well, Brody deserves it because he's so serious most of the time. I don't have any laundry for you. I have plenty of underwear."

"Are you sure because I certainly don't mind?"

"I'm sure, Joyce. I learned long ago that a woman can't pack too much underwear."

Joyce nods. "Oh, the stylist will be here at 3:00 tomorrow. Brody said you will leave around 6:00. Is that enough time?"

"Yes, that's plenty. Thanks for taking care of that for me. I hated to ask Brody."

"There's no telling what you would have gotten if you had asked Brody. He's never had to schedule a stylist before, much less even knows where to find one or what one is."

"Well, thanks again. I guess I better dress. Do you have any idea what he has in mind?"

"No, but I'm sure he'll have fun with you. Enjoy the day, Madison."

Madison quickly dresses in jeans, a polo shirt and sneakers. She goes downstairs to find Brody standing by the island, waiting for her.

"Is this okay?"

"That's perfect. Let's go."

Brody navigates the pickup through traffic, and soon they are on the interstate headed away from downtown. "I guess you think me spitting coffee all over the newspaper was funny," he says in a serious tone of voice.

"Brody, it was a much better reaction than I expected," Madison laughs.

"Are you?"

"Am I what?"

"You know." Brody looks over at Madison and raises his eyebrows. "Are you dressed, commando?"

"Oh, heck no. I have plenty of underwear. I was just teasing you."

Brody gives Madison a massive grin. "Well, I am because I didn't have any clean boxers, thanks to you." She rolls her eyes and punches him in the arm. Brody exits the interstate and soon pulls into the parking lot for the zoo.

"Oh, Brody. We're at the zoo," an excited Madison says, clapping her hands.

"I thought we could see it today. I doubt you would want to walk all over the zoo tomorrow night in high heels."

"Do you come here often?"

"I try to come when they have new or remodeled exhibits, but I've been so busy lately that I haven't had a chance."

"Well, sir will you please open my door, and let's go. I can't wait to see it."

Holding hands, the pair spends almost all day at the zoo. They laugh and try to imitate the animals. It reminds Madison of how excited Brody was at the fair. He is so relaxed and happy. I get the impression that there isn't much happiness in his life, she thinks. As a friend, I hope I can help with that. Leaving the zoo, the pair stop for a dinner of chili dogs followed by ice cream before returning home.

"Brody, thank you for a wonderful time," Madison says as they walk in the apartment's entry way.

"There's a game on tonight. Would you watch it with me?" Brody asks.

"Sure, but I want to change clothes first. I ate so much I think my jeans will burst open," Madison answers. She runs upstairs and returns in one of Brody's T-shirts and a pair of his socks.

Brody is seated on the sofa when she returns. "You must find my clothes comfortable," he says, looking up at her when she enters the room.

"They remind me of you," she unintentionally blurts out. Brody's facial expression is one of confusion. "Uh, they are very comfortable," Madison says quickly, trying to pretend she didn't say what she did. Brody looks away, and she walks to the opposite end of the sofa. Madison sits and pulls her knees up under her chin, wrapping her arms around her legs.

"Would you mind if I lay my head in your lap?" Brody asks.

"No, not at all."

He lies on his back and puts his head in her lap. "Madison, are you looking forward to the gala tomorrow night?"

"Yes, I am, and that reminds me to ask if you would go with me to a formal event next week?"

"Well, aren't we just the social butterflies this month?" Brody smirks.

Madison laughs and says "I guess we are, but this is my last one for several months."

"Mine, too so I'll have to put my tux into mothballs. What color is your dress? I need to see if I have a cummerbund to match."

"A cummerbund? Wow, this is formal isn't it? My dress is green, but I guess people would say emerald."

Brody reaches up, pushes a lock of Madison's hair behind her ear, and brushes her cheek with his fingers. "The color of your eyes," he says as he closes his eyes.

Brody's touch made Madison feel hot and tingly inside when he touched her. Unable to resist, she runs her fingers through Brody's thick salt and pepper hair. He opens his eyes, and they stare at each other for a few moments. Then he closes his eyes once more.

When Brody's breathing slows, and Madison knows he's asleep, she watches him, wondering how it would feel to have his full lips on hers. Heck, she ponders not just on her lips but all over her. Would it be making love with him or just sex? Would it be slow and gentle or fast and furious?

"A penny for your thoughts," a deep voice says, causing Madison to jump. Brody opens his eyes. They are so dark blue that she holds her breath before answering.

"I thought you were asleep," she finally says.

"Not yet. Well? Your thoughts?"

"No, Brody. I'd rather not share my thoughts right now. Go to sleep."

"Why not, Madison? Is it possible I was having the same thoughts as you?"

"I doubt it, Brody. I really doubt it," she sighs.

"You never know," Brody says smiling as he closes his eyes again and leaves his statement lingering in the air between them.

"I wish you were," Madison whispers.

Chapter 34

BRODY

"Good morning, Madison," Brody says as she walks into the kitchen. He notices she is dressed in capris and her own T-shirt. "Joyce is off today, but she left breakfast sandwiches in the fridge. I've eaten because I need to run errands this morning."

"Okay and please be careful," she says, walking past him to the fridge.

Brody stands, grabs his phone, and tells her he'll be back soon. Madison nods without looking at him.

Well, that was odd, he contemplates as he gets into the elevator. She's usually a bundle of energy. I wonder if she's thinking about our brief conversation last night when she wouldn't tell me her thoughts. I know my thoughts. I wanted to pull her head down and kiss the heck out of her. I bet her lips are as soft as her cheek. Thank goodness she didn't look any further than my face. That would have been embarrassing for both of us.

That woman knocks my world off its axis, and I don't know why. Sure, I'd like to have her in my bed, but there's something more to it than that. I wish I knew what it was.

Brody's first stop is a tuxedo store, where he purchases an emerald cummerbund. No, it's unnecessary, but for some reason unknown to him, everyone at the gala needs know they are together.

His next stop is a jewelry store where he buys gifts for his mother. She's the only woman he has ever bought jewelry for, but today he has something else in mind. Brody talks to the owner about renting a pair of earrings. Because he is a good customer, the owner agrees, and Brody finds a pair of exquisite diamond and emerald earrings. They are approximately two inches long, and the jewels are large enough to sparkle in any light.

Brody's last stop is a florist, where he purchases a vase filled with two dozen yellow roses for his mother. She and her husband returned home late last night and will attend the gala as well.

By the time Brody delivers the roses to his mother and has lunch with her and her husband, it is 2:50 before he returns to his apartment. Madison is nowhere to be found, so he assumes she is in her bedroom.

The intercom buzzes. "Mr. McGuire, I have a Pierre down here. He says he is here to see Ms. Donaldson."

"That's for me," Madison yells from the top of the stairs.

"Okay, send him up," Brody says with raised eyebrows.

Within two minutes, the elevator door opens. There stands Pierre holding a large suitcase. "Hello, sir. I'm here for Ms. Donaldson."

Confused, Brody points at the stairs. "She's in the first door on the left." Pierre nods and heads in that direction.

Brody watches the man and then says, "I wonder what Madison needs with Pierre. It must be a woman thing." He retreats to his office to catch up on emails before time to dress for the gala.

Looking at himself in the mirror, Brody muses that he's nervous as a cat on a hot tin roof. "I don't know why I'm so nervous," he mutters.

His reflection is the mirror smiles. You know why. You are taking a beautiful woman into a den filled with mostly vipers and witches. "I hope I'm not making a mistake," he says to the reflection. Brody's mind says you're not because Madison can hold her own.

Dressed in his full formal regalia, including his new emerald-colored cummerbund, Brody waits nervously for Madison to appear. Then, when he can take it no more, he goes to the kitchen and pours two fingers of bourbon to calm his nerves.

He takes a sip and hears, "I'm ready." He looks toward the stairs, and there stands a goddess in a strapless emerald gown. Her silver hair lays across her shoulders in waves. There's just the right amount of cleavage showing above the gown. The dress fits the goddess' curves perfectly. Brody stands mesmerized at the sight, watching the goddess ease her way down the stairs.

Madison stops at the bottom step and smiles. "Does this meet your approval, sir?"

Brody realizes he's been holding his breath, watching her float down the stairs. He clears his throat and states, "Madison, you are so beautiful. Let's just stay here and let me stare at you all night."

"I can assure you I wouldn't stay dressed like this all night if we stayed here," she replies, one corner of her mouth of her gorgeous red lips tilting upward. "Brody, you are so handsome it hurts my eyes to look at you."

Sitting his glass down on the island, Brody slowly walks toward Madison stopping mere inches from her. "I have something that will complete this outfit." He reaches into his pocket, pulls out a small bag, and hands it to her.

Madison takes the bag slowly, opens it, and turns it upside down in her palm. The diamond and emerald earrings fall into her hand. "Oh, my gosh, Brody. You shouldn't have."

"They are on loan for tonight. I saw them, and I knew they were perfect for you."

"Would you hold my wrap and purse so I can put them in?" Brody nods and reaches for the items. Once Madison has them in her ears, he places his hands on her shoulders and guides her to a full-length mirror in the foyer.

"I was right," Brody whispers in her ear, his hands still on her shoulders. "They are perfect, just like you." Madison's eyes meet his in the mirror, and something passes between them. Something deep and almost mysterious.

Brody places a tender kiss on her shoulder and looks back at the mirror. He hears Madison moan as she leans her head back. I could rip this dress off her and make her mine this moment. But he backs up, so Madison doesn't feel his body react to her. Finally, he clears his throat and says, "we better go."

He sees what appears to be disappointment in Madison's eyes, but she turns around rapidly and reaches for the wrap and purse Brody had tucked under his arm. She places the wrap around her shoulders and tells him she's ready.

George is waiting for Brody and Madison at the curb. George opens Madison's door and tells her she looks beautiful. She smiles and thanks him as Brody helps her into the back seat.

The ride is silent to the gala. Brody watches Madison out of the corner of his eye, wondering what she is thinking as she looks out the window. He wills his body to calm down before they reach the zoo. Thank goodness this jacket is long, or it would be pretty embarrassing for me.

Once they arrive, Brody helps Madison out of the SUV and offers her his arm. She tentatively takes it but doesn't look at him. He leads her down the red carpet into a massive tent with three adjoining tents. A man approaches them, and Madison suddenly transforms into the perfect date, which pleases Brody greatly.

When Brody introduces her to various people, Madison smiles, shakes hands, and chats with the people. While one woman talks about dresses, Brody leaves Madison's side to get drinks. When he turns to go back to her, Ted is talking to Madison. Brody watches Ted move closer and closer to Madison while she continuously backs up. Brody hurries back to her, and Ted sees him coming and quickly disappears into the crowd.

"Are you okay?" Brody asks, handing Madison her drink.

"I'm fine, but Ted makes me nervous and I don't know why."

Brody nods and says, "let's go find our table." He leads Madison to a table at the front of the tent, where the board of directors will sit. Unfortunately, Madison is to be seated next to Ben. Brody notices her frown when she sees the seating arrangement. He looks around and switches the place cards so he is sitting beside Ben instead. When Madison looks at Brody in surprise, he winks at her, and for the first time since the encounter in the foyer, she smiles directly at him.

As the rest of the table guests join them, Brody introduces Madison. She recognizes two of the couples from the fundraiser in Pineville and Ben. Then, dinner is served, and an auction takes place afterward. Brody drapes his arm over the back of Madison's chair feeling the heat of her body and deeply inhaling her unique scent when the auction begins.

Brody bids on a set of golf clubs, but he doesn't win, which is fine because he already has a set and doesn't like golf that much. When a deep sea fishing trip off the Florida coast is up, Brody bids and finally wins at $35,000. Next up for auction is a week's stay at a plush island resort Brody has donated. It sells for $50,000 and Madison can tell he is pleased the donation went for such a high price.

When the auction is over, the music begins. The crowd is invited to dance. Madison excuses herself to go to the restroom while Brody waits for her at the table. After a while, she returns, and he leads her onto the dance floor. As Brody places his hand on Madison's hip, he feels tension in her body. He pulls her close and holds her tightly against him. Madison feels so good in his arms that he could dance with her forever.

As the song changes, Brody spies his mother and her husband across the room. "Madison, I'd like to introduce you to my mother and her husband," he tells her and she nods. He offers her his hand, but she refuses, placing her hand on his arm instead. That's strange, he thinks.

After the introductions, Brody's mother talks to Madison while Brody talks to her husband. Several women walk by and smile seductively at Brody, but he ignores them.

After several more dances, Brody can still feel Madison's tension, so he asks her if she is ready to go. She answers yes, and he texts George to bring the car to the entrance.

Midway to the apartment, Madison looks over at Brody and breaks the silence of the ride. "Who's Lauren?"

Brody is taken aback by the question and says, "why do you ask?"

"She was in the restroom talking to two other women and she didn't know I was in there."

"Lauren is just a woman I know. Sometimes, she has been my plus one to events."

"Well, listening to her talk, she considers herself more than your plus one," Madison states, feeling suddenly jealous.

"If that's how she feels, I can assure you it's one-sided. Lauren is a trust fund baby whose trust fund is quickly evaporating. She's looking for a rich husband."

"Okay," Madison says, looking out the front window.

Brody takes a deep breath. "Let me put it this way. Lauren has been convenient when I needed female company." Madison nods and is quiet the rest of the way.

"Would you like a drink?" Brody asks as they walk into the apartment.

"No, thank you. I'm tired, so I'll just go to bed."

"Would you like me to unzip you?"

"No, I can manage," Madison answers as she walks toward the stairs. Brody watches her, wondering what made this night a total screw-up. I hoped Madison would have a lovely time, but something upset her. I must figure out if it was me or if something happened at the gala.

Chapter 35

BRODY

Unable to sleep, Brody is up before sunrise. When he slept, he dreamed of the goddess in the emerald dress. When he was awake, which was most of the night, Brody wondered about Madison and the change in her demeanor last night.

By the time Madison appears fully dressed, he has finished an entire pot of coffee. Brody can tell she slept little because of the dark circles under her eyes. "Good morning," he says.

"Good morning, Brody," Madison replies walking to the coffee pot and putting on a pot to brew.

Before he can say anything else, the elevator door opens. Since Brody isn't expecting anyone, he rushes around the corner to see who it is.

"Lauren! How did you find me, and more importantly, how did you get up here?"

"Hello, Brody. I just came from visiting your mother. She told me you lived here and gave me the code."

"Why are you even here?"

"I came to explain that you made a fool out of yourself last night."

"How's that, Lauren?" Brody asks.

"Bringing that old woman as your date. Brody, she's mature enough to be your mother. How could you do that to me? You know I always go to the gala with you. I was so embarrassed."

"Is this about my date, or is this about you?" Brody asks in an angry voice.

"It's about you, Brody," Lauren screams. "You embarrassed yourself, me, and your mother. What is that old woman to you, anyway?"

"Lauren, get out of my apartment," Brody yells back. "Who I take to events is my business, not my mother's, and certainly not yours. I won't discuss my relationships with you. Now, get out, and never come back."

"I'm sorry, Brody," Lauren cries, but Brody can tell it's fake. "You know I just want what's best for you and hanging around with someone old enough to be your mother isn't it."

"Lauren, I said go, or would you rather I call security and have you escorted out of the building?"

"I'll go, but you know where to find me, Brody. I'll be waiting for you like I always do."

Brody walks to the elevator, pushes the button, and opens the elevator door immediately.

Lauren steps into the car and says, "Brody, please. Please don't treat me this way. You know how I feel about you."

Brody pushes the button, and the doors close. Then he pushes the intercom button next to the elevator.

"Yes, Mr. McGuire?" a woman answers in a professional voice.

"Please change my elevator code immediately and make sure that blond woman getting off the elevator never sets foot in this building again. That includes visiting my mother as well."

"Yes, Mr. McGuire. I'll change the code right now and text it to you."

Brody runs his fingers over his strong jaw and turns around. There stands Madison. He looks at her and can tell by her expression she heard every word. He sees the pain in her eyes, and a tear runs down her cheek, which she quickly brushes away.

"Please take me home now," she says, running up the stairs.

"Madison, wait," Brody yells at her, but she doesn't stop. Dammit, what do I do now, he thinks running his fingers through his hair?

The ride to Pineville is eerily quiet. When Brody pulls into Madison's driveway, he turns to her and says, "Madison, I'm so sorry."

"It's okay, Brody. Lauren said nothing I didn't already know. Besides, I heard it all last night in the restroom."

"Do you still want me to go with you Saturday night?" he asks quietly.

"Yes, I wish you would. At least no one around here is that judgmental. I'll text you the time to pick me up." Madison gets out of the pickup and walks to her door. Brody gets her suitcase and dress bag out of the car.

"Can I come in?" he asks when he reaches her door.

"I don't think so, Brody because I need some time alone." He sets the suitcase down and hands her the dress bag. Madison looks at him. "Be safe going home." As he watches, she picks up the suitcase, walks into the house, and closes the door.

Brody slowly walks to the pickup and gets in. As he buckles his seatbelt, he feels terrible and angry. The last thing Brody ever wanted was for this precious woman to be hurt, and in less than twenty-four hours, Lauren hurt Madison twice. Maybe I hurt her too, he thinks.

As he drives back to Knoxville, Brody replays every moment in his mind searching for answers. From the time Madison walked down the stairs looking so delicious to when she shut the door practically in his face.

By the time Brody gets home, the only thing he's decided on is that he does not know what to say to comfort Madison when she gets hurt. Joyce looks up at him when he walks past her. Brody goes straight to the liquor cabinet, grabs two bottles of bourbon, and heads to his bedroom. The velvet bag with the earrings lies in the center of his bed.

132

Chapter 36

MADISON

Madison drops the suitcase in the middle of the living room floor and throws the dress bag on the sofa. However, she carefully sets her tote down only because she doesn't want to break the laptop. Madison walks like a zombie to her bedroom and falls across her bed, sobbing.

"Madison. Madison." She turns over to find Bruce standing over her. "You look like death warmed over," he says, seeing her red face and swollen eyes.

"What are you doing here?"

"I've been calling and texting you all afternoon. I finally called Brody, and he said he brought you home around noon."

"What else did he say?" she asks.

"Nothing and that's why I came over to check on you. Get off that bed because I brought two bottles of that red wine you like. You can tell me what's going on then." Madison gets up, goes to the bathroom, and washes her face while Bruce goes to the kitchen.

When she walks into the living room, Bruce sits on the sofa with two glasses and two open bottles of wine. "Sit down beside me and tell your old friend, Bruce, what's happened."

First, Madison tells Bruce about overhearing Lauren's conversation with two women in the bathroom and Lauren's conversation with Brody that morning. Next, she tells Bruce about the moment between her and Brody before the gala.

When she finishes, and one bottle of wine is empty, Bruce says, "what do you think?"

"I think Lauren is right because I'm at least ten years older than Brody. I'm too old to be his friend, much less anything else. I certainly don't want to embarrass him in front of his mother and his friends."

Bruce reaches for Madison's hand and asks, "what about that moment the two of you shared?"

"Bruce, I don't know. To me, it seemed very special somehow. Sometimes I feel he wants to touch or kiss me, but he quickly backs away." Madison pours another glass of wine for each of them.

"You're falling for him, aren't you?" Bruce says, squeezing her hand.

"I'm afraid I am. Brody's so close to my vision of an ideal man for me, but I'm too old for him, and he knows it. He's probably just leading me on, teasing me." Tears roll down Madison's cheeks.

Bruce wipes the tears away and lifts her chin so she has to look at him. "Madison, I don't think he's teasing you. I saw the way he looked at you at the fundraiser. Several beautiful, single women there could have caught his attention, but he only had eyes for you. When you danced, it was as if you were the only two people in the room. I also don't believe he's the kind of man to lead you on."

"He was just being kind at the fundraiser because I invited him."

"Whatever, but I stand behind my observation. Is Brody still going with you Saturday night?"

"Yes, I asked him to because I thought it would be rude to cancel this late."

"Madison, has Brody ever been married or in love?" Bruce asks.

"He's never been married, but told me he was engaged twice. He said the first time, the woman broke up with him because she told him she didn't love him. He broke off the engagement the second time because the woman was after his money and name."

Bruce studies Madison for a few seconds. "Madison, did you know Brody is a very wealthy man?"

She shrugs and says, "no, but I guess he is. I know he owns his business, whatever that is. His apartment is enormous, and he owns at least three cars. That's all I know and I don't care to learn more because it's not important to me. We talked about our ideal man/woman the other night. Brody said his ideal woman would have many of the same qualities my ideal man would have. So I asked him if he's ever met his ideal woman."

"What did he say?" Bruce asks in a serious voice.

"He brought up one woman has come close, but he's still learning about her," Madison replies.

"That's interesting and hang onto that thought a minute." Bruce gets up and returns from the kitchen with another bottle of wine. He opens up his phone and makes a call. "Hi, sweetheart and yes I've had too much wine, so I'm going to stay at Madison's tonight." Bruce listens for a minute. "Yeah, okay. Love you too." He hangs up and pours them another glass of wine.

"What did Perry have to say?"

"He said he didn't care how long I was gone or how much wine I drank. He wants me to stay until you feel better. So, Brody mentioned one woman has come close. I find that very interesting."

Madison looks at him. "Interesting in what way?"

"So just hear me out or the wine, whichever is talking right now," Bruce says. "From what you told me, Brody said, he might never have been in love, so maybe he's confused."

"Confused about what?"

"I don't know for sure. It could be his feelings or his emotions or both. He told you Lauren was convenient. That means convenient for sex. So maybe he's getting his feelings mixed up with sexual desire. On the other hand, you have been in love, so you know what those feelings are like and you know the difference. You know how powerful they can be and destructive. Why not wait and see how Saturday night goes?"

Madison ponders his question. "I'll try, but I just know when he looks at me or touches me, I get all warm and wet."

Bruce laughs, "you're not too old for love and a good romp in the old bed. Now, we've finished the third bottle of wine so I'm going to bed. Goodnight, my sweet friend." Bruce kisses Madison on the forehead and walks to the spare bedroom. "It's okay to dream about Brody. It's also okay to fantasize about him." Bruce laughs and closes the bedroom door.

Madison carries the empty wine bottles and glasses to the kitchen and heads to bed. Maybe Bruce is right. I'll see how the week and Saturday night go.

Chapter 37

BRODY

Brody wakes Monday morning with a horrendous headache. He's in his bed but still dressed and covered with a blanket. *I guess Joyce covered me up after I passed out.* He looks at the clock on his nightstand. It is 10:00. *Dammit, I should have been at work an hour ago.* Next to his clock is a glass of Joyce's hangover remedy, which tastes awful, two ibuprofen, a cup of hot coffee, and two slices of dry toast. The hangover mixture tastes horrible, but Brody knows it works.

He quickly downs the remedy, eats the toast, takes the ibuprofen, and drinks the coffee. He lies down for a few minutes letting the mixture and the ibuprofen do its magic. As his headache eases, Brody gets off the bed. strips, and heads for the shower. The hot water feels great on his aching body. Finally dressed after skipping his shaving routine, Brody lets George drive him to work.

"Don't you look like something a cat dragged in? I bet you feel like it too," Angela greets him. Brody rolls his eyes at her, walks directly into his office, and slams the door closed. Angela has a cup of hot coffee waiting for him on his desk.

Brody sits down and puts his head in his hands. What a mess he's in, and he has no one to ask for advice. There's Angela, but does he really want to get that deep into his private life? I might not have a choice unless I want to go to a therapist. I'm already paying Angela, he smirks. Unable to sit still, Brody carries his coffee to the window and looks out.

There's a soft knock on his door. Brody turns as Angela opens the door. "Do you need another cup of coffee?" she asks.

"That would be nice since I let this one get cold."

"Okay. I'll be right back with a hot one." Two minutes later, Angela's back with a fresh cup. "Do you want to talk about it?" she says.

Brody takes the offered cup and hands her the cold one. "I do, and I don't."

"You can tell me the part you're comfortable with if you like. You know I'm a good listener."

"Well, I'll tell you the worst part." Brody draws a deep breath and sits in his chair. "It starts and ends with Lauren."

"That selfish, spoiled witch? What did she do this time?"

Brody tells Angela about Lauren's visit to his apartment yesterday morning. He recounts everything Lauren said while Madison was in the kitchen and heard everything. After he kicked her out and apologized to Madison, Madison admitted she had overheard Lauren having the same conversation in the restroom. "It appears Madison is very sensitive about our age difference even though I told her early on it didn't matter to me."

"How old is she, Brody?"

"I honestly don't know. Lauren said Madison is old enough to be my mother, but I'm sure she's not that old, and she certainly doesn't look that old. She has silver hair and tiny wrinkles around her eyes though."

"How do you know she has tiny wrinkles around her eyes?" Angela asks, thoughtfully.

"Madison took a nap with her head in my lap one afternoon and I watched her sleep."

"Why did you watch her?"

"I don't know why, Angela. She was so beautiful, and she looked like an angel lying there. I couldn't help myself and I missed most of the football game because of it."

Angela contemplates his answer for a few seconds. Then she says, "I have a question you need to ask yourself. Are you lusting after Madison, or are you having real feelings for her? Regardless of your answer, send her a message, so she knows you're thinking about her today. That might make both of you feel better. Now you have a 1:00 meeting with Mike in the conference room to complete the proposal he's been working on."

"You should be in the meeting too since I'm not focusing very well today." Angela nods and leaves softly, closing the door behind her. She's right. I should message Madison, but what do I say?

Brody leans his head back and closes his eyes for a few minutes picturing Madison walking down the stairs in that emerald gown Saturday night. She was almost glowing and looked like a goddess. Every man at the gala noticed her. He remembers the two of them looking in the mirror. Something passed between them, and they both knew it, but what was it?

I should have never kissed her on the shoulder. Or maybe, I shouldn't have backed away when I heard her moan. I've never heard a woman moan like that before. So what was it Madison said when we were talking about our ideal partner? Something about her ideal man would listen to her gasps and moans to pick up how to satisfy her. It was when I backed away that her whole demeanor changed. I bet she thinks I'm toying with her and I can see where she might get that impression. If she only knew how much I wanted her at that moment. But as Angela asked, is it lust or genuine feelings? I just don't know, and that scares me.

Angela interrupts his thoughts by announcing on the intercom that the meeting is in fifteen minutes. Brody grabs his phone and types the message, "I seriously miss you and everything about you." He rereads the message. That sounds little adolescent, but it's how I feel, he decides. He hits the send button and leaves his office for the conference room.

Chapter 38

MADISON

Something wakes Madison up, but the noise doesn't register. Her head hurts, her body aches, and her stomach is queasy. Then, she hears the sound again and realizes someone is ringing the doorbell. Madison hears voices and eases out of bed, stumbling to the living area.

"What idiot rings a doorbell at this time of the morning?" she mumbles.

"It's almost noon, and an idiot that delivers his home remedy for hangovers." Madison looks up to find a smiling Perry standing in the kitchen with a thermos. Bruce is already gulping a glass of the concoction. Perry grabs a glass off the counter, pours something red into it, and hands it to Madison. "Drink it all, and then another glass full. I guarantee it works."

"What's in it?" Madison asks.

"Don't ask. Just drink it fast," Bruce says, handing his glass to Perry for a refill. Madison does as she's told and almost turns green. Then she sets the glass down, and Perry refills it.

"Are you trying to kill us?" Madison says, making Perry laugh. She does, however, gulp the second glass.

"Okay, now both of you go sit on the sofa and wait," Perry says. So they sit down, and seconds later, Perry appears with water and ibuprofen for each of them, which they gladly take. Bruce lies his head in Madison's lap, and she leans her head back. Both fall asleep almost instantly.

Bruce wakes first and moves, waking Madison. "Did we go to bed last night?" Madison asks. Bruce nods. "Did I dream Perry was here?"

"No, he was here with his magic potion. How do you feel?" Bruce says.

"Not bad at all. What about you?"

"I feel pretty good, but I think we better stick with only two bottles of wine in the future."

Madison giggles and says, "I agree. Did we get anything solved?" Then, she hears her phone ping with a message. "Where's my phone?"

Bruce looks around. "I don't know, but I'll call the phone so we can find it." He dials her number, and they hear it ring on the other side of the room.

"It's still in my tote." Madison gets the tote and retrieves her phone. "It's a message from Brody."

"What's it say?" Bruce asks.

"He says he misses me and everything about me."

"That sounds promising so answer him back."

"What should I say, Bruce?"

"Just say that you miss him and you're sorry you ruined his weekend."

"That's simple enough." Madison types her message. "Okay, here's what I wrote. I miss your smile, your conversation and your underwear. I'm sorry I ruined the weekend, and I promise to do better next weekend."

Bruce studies her. "Okay, send it and then explain the underwear part."

Madison presses send and then tells Bruce about wearing Brody's underwear and her thought about going commando. They laugh until tears run down their cheeks, and Madison gets the hiccups.

Finally, Bruce says, "Madison, I've got to go. Are you sure I'll see you and Brody Saturday night?"

"You will see me for sure. Brody said he would go, but he might still cancel."

Bruce kisses her cheek. "He'll be there, Madison because he can't resist spending time with you."

After Bruce leaves, Madison unpacks, does laundry, and works on her latest project until bedtime.

Chapter 39

BRODY

Even though the alarm went off minutes ago, Brody remains in bed. He picks up his phone and reads Madison's message for probably the one-hundredth time. She sent the message during his meeting with Mike. Brody choked on his coffee when he read she missed his underwear. Mike jumped up and wanted to do the Heimlich maneuver on him.

An idea develops in his head, so he jumps out of bed, showers, shaves and dresses for the day. Joyce is making his breakfast when he walks into the kitchen.

"Joyce, I need a very important favor today."

"Sure, Mr. McGuire."

"Do you know anyone that does embroidery?"

"Actually I do it in my spare time. What do you have in mind?"

"You're going to think I'm crazy, but that's okay because I might be. You remember Madison wearing my underwear?" Joyce giggles and nods. "Would you buy seven pairs of boxers, socks, and seven T-shirts in seven different matching colors? Next, embroider the days of the week on all of them and then, send them to Madison by courier?"

"Oh my, Mr. McGuire. That's hilarious and I'll do it this morning and have them delivered tomorrow. Do you want to add a message?"

"I don't think I need to, do you, Joyce?"

"No, sir. I think the gift will speak for itself. Now, sit down and eat while your food is hot. Just leave everything, and I'll clean it up when I return. I have a critical errand to run." Joyce pats Brody on the shoulder and leaves.

Smiling, Brody picks up his phone and types a message to Madison. "Have to leave tomorrow and won't be back until late Friday. What time should I pick you up Saturday, and is it (ugh) black tie again?" He presses send and gets an instant reply.

"Not black tie, but after 5:00 apparel. It starts at 7:30, so please pick me up at 7:00."

Then another message, "Travel safely and good luck!"

Well, not a black-tie event, but a suit. That's much better, Brody decides. I wonder what Madison will wear. I can't wait to see her.

Chapter 40

BRODY

Brody arrives at the cabin at 9:00 am Saturday. He fishes until 4:00 and gets cleaned up for that night's event. Brody hasn't heard from Madison since Tuesday. He thought she might message him about the underwear, but she didn't. Joyce assured him the package was delivered on Wednesday.

As he dresses, Brody decides tonight will be a fantastic night for both of them. He will see that nothing goes wrong. Madison deserves a great night after last weekend.

Brody pulls into Madison's driveway at 6:58, walks to the door, and rings the bell. Madison answers, wearing a silver dress with a round neckline and three-quarter-length sleeves. Brody notices the dress hits her right above the knees showing off her fantastic calves.

"Hi, Brody. Come in. We have time for a quick drink so would you like one?"

"I would. You look great, Madison."

She curtsies and beams. "Thanks. This dress goes well with my new underwear."

146

"Really? You got new underwear? I'd love to see it sometime." Madison punches him on the arm and leads the way to the kitchen. She pours him a bourbon and a glass of wine for herself. "So what's tonight's event for?" Brody asks.

"This is for the local animal shelter and it's at the country club. Nothing fancy, just dinner and dancing. Oh, and of course, the usual boring speech."

"There's no auction or anything exciting?"

"No, the cost of the tickets was the donations. You look very handsome tonight." Brody bows low showing off his broad shoulders. He did not know what Madison was wearing, but he made a good choice wearing his dark gray suit, light gray shirt and maroon tie."

"We're almost twins, aren't we?" he says gazing at her from top to bottom. "How far is the drive to the country club?"

"It's about ten minutes drive, so we better be going," Madison answers.

The evening is perfect in Brody's mind. The food was good, but holding Madison in his arms as they danced was even better. That is until Ted tried to cut in and dance with Madison. That's when she said she needed to go to the restroom. Ted didn't ask again, so Brody had Madison all to himself except for Bruce and Perry. Madison is so relaxed tonight, and I'm so thankful, Brody thinks as he watches Bruce lead her around the dance floor.

On the drive to Madison's house, the pair talk about the dinner and how much more fun it was since it wasn't as formal as the other events they attended together. Finally, Brody asks Madison if he could take her to breakfast the following morning, and she agrees.

Brody walks her to the door and goes inside for a nightcap before heading to the cabin and bed. When she walks him to the door, she kisses him on the cheek and thanks him for going with her.

Chapter 41

MADISON

About five minutes after Brody leaves, Madison's doorbell rings. Thinking it is Brody, she opens the door without checking to see who it is. She is shocked to find Ted standing at the door.

"Ted! What are you doing here and how did you find out where I live?"

"I followed you home. Man, I thought Brody would never leave." Ted walks in without being invited.

Madison gets an extremely bad feeling and turns her back on Ted to close the door. Fortunately, she has her phone in her hand and presses the record button. "What do you want, Ted?"

"I want what you've been giving to Brody and Ben for free, you whore." Ted lunges for Madison, but she dodges him and moves swiftly to put the sofa between the two of them. "Oh, so you want to play," Ted says with a smile. "I like to play." He rushes around the sofa. Madison stumbles in her heels, and Ted grabs her. He throws her over the back of the sofa and onto the cushions. Then he dives on top of her.

Madison struggles to get out from under him, but Ted's weight is too much. She tosses the phone down on the floor next to her. "Ted, let me up now," Madison demands.

"No, I see what I need, and I want you. We can make this the easy way or the hard way, Madison. It's all up to you."

"No, Ted. You've got it all wrong. Brody and I don't have that kind of relationship."

"You're lying. I've seen the way the two of you look at each other. Two lovers gazing into each other's eyes. It makes me sick to my stomach. He's not your kind of man. I am."

"Ted, please let me go. What about Brody? He's your friend?"

"Not until I've had my fill of you. Besides, Brody and I share women. You know who Lauren is."

Madison's phone rings and she struggles to look down at it. "It's Brody so I better answer it."

"Okay, but don't you dare tell him I'm here." Ted leans back, so he is sitting on her thighs.

Madison grabs the phone and answers it. "Hi, Brody."

"Madison, I forgot to ask you what time I should pick you up in the morning."

"Oh, Brody. I know you left some things here. Will you pick them up in the morning on your way home?"

"Uh, Madison. Are you okay?" Brody asks, confused.

"No, it's no problem. I'll gather them up and have them ready for you."

"Madison, are you in trouble?"

"Yes, donuts sound good. The chocolate-covered ones are my favorite."

"Madison, can you call 911?"

"No, I'm exhausted and getting ready for bed," she says.

"I'll call them, and I'm on my way." Brody hangs up immediately.

"What did he want?" Ted demands as Madison lays the phone face down on the table next to the sofa.

"He forgot some things and will pick them up in the morning," Madison answers.

"You lying bitch." Ted strikes her across the face. "I'll teach you to lie to me." He continues to hit Madison in the face and punch her hard in the side. The harder she struggles, the harder Ted hits her. Madison fights back as best she can until one blow to her side nearly blinds her with pain. She knows her ribs broke because she heard the crack.

Ted grabs the neck of her dress and tugs it hard and Madison feels it tear apart. Tired of Madison's fists pounding at him, Ted pins her wrists down with one hand and rips off her bra and underwear with the other. Madison tries to use her hips and legs to buck Ted off, but it doesn't work.

He leans over and bites her hard above her right breast. "That will be a reminder for you of our romantic night together." Then, Ted continues to hit her about the face and body. Madison feels one of her eyes swelling shut and finally stops struggling.

"Good girl," Ted's hot breath fills her ear as he leans over her. "I should have known you like it rough. Now I know Brody's not the right man for you because he's not into rough."

Suddenly, the front door flies open. Two police officers run in, grab Ted, and pull him off Madison. Right behind them is Brody. "Brody," Madison whispers when she sees him and then blacks out.

Chapter 42

BRODY

"**I** can't see and I can't move!" Madison's screams loudly waking Brody. He jumps off his bed and goes to her where she's shaking all over.

"Madison, baby. Everything is going to be okay," he murmurs in her ear as he sits beside her on the bed.

"Brody?" she cries.

"Yes, baby. I'm right here with you," he says, grabbing her hand.

"Brody, I can't see or move." He hears the terror in her voice.

"Baby, it's okay for now because your eyes are swollen. Once the swelling goes down in a day or two, you'll be able to see fine. Your hands are tied so you wouldn't pull out the IV when reaching for your eyes."

"Are you absolutely sure, Brody?"

He wipes her tears away gently. "Do you trust me, Madison?" She nods her answer. "Good because I wouldn't lie to you about something important like that."

"Where am I? Am I in a hospital?"

"No, baby. You're in my apartment with me. I brought you here so I can keep you safe."

151

"I'm so scared, Brody. Does Ted know I'm here? Can he get to me?" Madison shakes again and reaches out for Brody.

Brody stands and carefully climbs onto the bed beside her. "I'm trying to be careful and not hurt you," he says, lying beside her. Brody raises her head enough to slide his arm underneath it. Then he lays his arm across her hips. "Does that hurt, Madison?" She shakes her head slightly and reaches down for his arm.

"Now, I'm going to hold you and make you feel safe while I answer your questions. Ted doesn't know you're here. The only ones who know you're here are George and Joyce, Bruce and Perry, the police and your nurse, Jane.

"My nurse?"

"Yes, you need medical attention for a few days, and Jane will take care of you. It's okay because she's a close friend of Joyce's. Ted is out of jail on bond, but he can't leave his home. He couldn't get to you if he wanted to because I've hired a security team to guard you and the building. They are here in the apartment and downstairs at all times. When I'm not with you, Jane and a female security officer will be. You don't have to worry, baby. Do you remember I told you I'd take care of you when we were at the Ferris wheel? I meant it. I will do everything in my power to protect you."

Madison feels Brody's whiskers against her cheek. "You need to shave and shower," she whispers.

Brody chuckles and says, "I know, but I was waiting for you to wake up."

"Hi, Madison. I'm Jane, your nurse. I'll stay with you while Mr. McGuire showers and shaves."

Brody laughs. "I can tell when I'm being dismissed. But, baby, will you be okay while I'm gone?" he whispers in her ear. Madison nods, and Brody climbs off the bed. He bends over and places a gentle kiss on her forehead. "I won't be gone long." He walks into his bathroom, but before he closes the door, he hears Madison.

"Jane, did Ted rape me?"

"No, he did not. Mr. McGuire and the police got there just in time. From what I've been told, Mr. McGuire hasn't left your side except for the emergency room and the ambulance on the drive here. He even had a bed moved in here so he could sleep close to you."

Madison thinks for several seconds and then says, "I didn't think the spare bedroom was big enough for another bed."

"Oh, my dear," Jane says. "You're in Mr. McGuire's bedroom, not the spare bedroom. Now, I'm going to give you something to relax you. It would be best if you lay still since you have three broken ribs on your left side. You also have a catheter."

"Okay. I wish Brody would lie down with me when he's finished. He makes me feel safe."

Brody eases the door closed. When Brody steps into the shower, all the feelings and emotions of the past two days overtake him. He hasn't cried since he was a small child, but now he sobs his heart out. Madison was severely hurt and almost raped. He wasn't around to protect her from Ted, a man Brody thought was his friend. But what kind of friend am I to Madison? Friends take care of friends, and I didn't. Can she forgive me for not being there for her?

After his shower and shaving, Brody opens the door and walks to Madison's bedside where she appears to be sleeping.

"Brody, I know you're close by."

"How did you know? I was trying to be quiet and not wake you."

"I'm not asleep. I smell your cologne and body wash."

Brody grins at Madison even though she can't see him. "Really? What do I smell like?"

"Your cologne is one of my favorites and I would recognize it any-where. Your body wash smells woodsy. It's almost like the fragrance of the woods at the cabin."

"So, if I wanted to sneak up on you, I need to be dirty and not shave?"

Madison smiles. "Probably so. I'm tired, Brody so would you lie down beside me while I take a nap? I feel safe knowing you're nearby."

Brody clambers onto the bed next to her nodding to Jane, signaling she is free to leave the room. Once Jane is out of the room, Brody says, "Madison, I'm so sorry I wasn't there to protect you from Ted. I should have asked if I could stay the night at your house."

Madison lifts her hand and caresses his face. "Brody, you have nothing to be sorry for. There's no way you could have known Ted would do something like that. I'm the one that should be sorry. I should have looked through the peephole. I thought you forgot something because it was so soon after you left." Madison yawns and closes her eyes quickly falling asleep. Brody rises slightly and softly kisses her full lips before falling asleep himself.

Chapter 43

BRODY

Brody looks down at Madison. It has taken two days for the swelling to go down enough that she can see. Her face is covered in bruises, but now a yellowish tint replaces all purple, black, and blue. Jane removed the catheter and IV yesterday and helped Madison to the bathroom several times.

"I'm hungry, Jane," Madison says. "I want no more broth. I want actual food."

"Madison, you need broth one more day," Jane replies.

"I feel like I'm being punished by having broth all the time."

Brody laughs and leaves the room for a few minutes. When he returns, he says, "Madison, there's a detective and prosecutor here to see you. Do you think you are up to talking to them?"

Madison looks up at him. "Yes, let's get this over with." Brody nods and leaves the room again. Soon he returns with two men that introduce themselves as Detective Marks and Assistant District Attorney Spencer.

Det. Marks speaks first. "Ms. Donaldson, you look much better than the other day I was here. Are you up to answering a few questions?"

As he stands behind the two men, Brody asks, "Madison, do you want me to leave the room?"

"No, Brody. Stay with me, please. Go ahead, Det. Marks, but my memory of that night is a little sketchy, though."

"Ms. Donaldson, first, let me say that was a great idea that you had to turn the recording feature on your phone to record the attack."

"What?" Brody nearly yells.

Det. Marks looks from Madison to Brody. "Mr. McGuire, when Ms. Donaldson answered the door and saw it wasn't you, she pressed the recording button. So everything that was said was recorded, including her phone call with you."

Brody can't believe his ears. Madison was such a genius to do that. He looks at her with amazement and admiration.

"Ms. Donaldson, although we can hear everything, we need you to tell us what happened. Are you up to listening to the recording?" Madison looks tentatively at Brody while he studies her eyes.

Madison then looks over to the Detective. "I'll do it, but I would like Brody to leave the room." She looks at Brody. "Brody, if you want to hear it, that's okay, but I need you to do it from another room. I can't bear to see you while I relive the attack."

Tears form in Brody's eyes because he knows what's on the recording is terrible. He nods, walks over to Madison, kisses her forehead, and leaves the room.

"Ready?" Det. Marks asks as Madison makes a deep breath and nods.

Brody wants to hear, and he doesn't. As he walks to the door, he is still trying to understand why Ted did what he did. Once outside the door, Brody leans against the wall and listens as Det. Marks starts the recording, and Brody listens.

"What do you want, Ted?" Madison says.

Then Ted calls Madison a whore who's been giving herself to Brody and Ben.

Brody hears the struggle, and Madison explains what happened. Then he hears Ted say he needs and wants Madison. Ted then says it can easy or hard. It's Madison's choice.

Madison tells Ted he's got the wrong idea. She and Brody aren't in that kind of relationship.

Next, Brody hears Ted say, "you're lying." Then Ted talks about how he and Madison look at each other. Ted refers to them as two lovers and says it makes him sick how they look at each other. He tells Madison that Brody's isn't her kind of man.

"Ted, please let me go. What about Brody? He's your friend," Madison's pleading voice on the recording fills Brody's ears and head. But when he hears Ted say, "not until I get my fill of you. Besides, Brody and I share our women. I know you know who Lauren is."

Brody feels his stomach turn inside out. He runs down the hall into the bathroom and retches. The next few minutes he spends on his knees sobbing and gagging. Finally, after a while, Brody washes his face and returns to Madison's doorway.

The room is deathly quiet. Brody peeks around the door and sees Madison quietly crying. "May I come in?" he asks. Madison looks up and motions for him to stand beside her bed.

"Okay, now what?" Madison wipes her tears away and then reaches for Brody's hand. He takes hers, giving it a gentle squeeze, and sits beside her on the bed.

It's ADA Spencer's turn to speak. "Mr. Weber was very pompous and denied everything initially, even though he was caught in the act. He said you have been flirting with him and leading him on at various charity functions both of you have attended." Brody jumps off the bed, but the ADA holds his hand up.

"Once he was told about the recording and heard it himself, his lawyer immediately began talking about a deal. Apparently, Mr. Weber is quite wealthy and well-known here in Knoxville. He doesn't want any publicity. So far, we've kept his and your names out of the news. Mr. Weber also doesn't want a trial, which is good for you, Ms. Donaldson."

"That figures," Brody says, disgusted. "Ted is only concerned about himself. Did he ever say he was sorry?" Madison squeezes his hand, knowing Brody is beyond angry.

ADA Spencer shakes his head. "Mr. Weber will pay all your medical expenses and future expenses related to the attack. He has volunteered to sell his home and business and move to another state if he can serve any prison time there. However, because of the violent nature of the crime, we offered fifteen years in prison with no possibility of parole. He is required by law to register as a sex offender." The ADA pauses briefly. "Mr. Weber's attorney countered the offer with fifteen years with the possibility of parole after ten years followed by five years probation. I need to hear your opinion, Ms. Donaldson."

Everyone looks at Madison. Brody can see the tiny wrinkles form between her eyebrows, which means she is thinking very hard. No one says a word for several minutes.

Finally, Madison looks at the ADA. "Mr. Weber's attorney deal is good, but I have a few stipulations. First, Mr. Weber is never to return to Tennessee or Kentucky or own a business in the states. Second, I want him to serve in a real prison environment, not a country club facility. Third, I also want him to attend anger management classes and finally, I want a formal written apology to me and one to Brody."

"That's unnecessary, Madison," Brody says.

"Yes, I think it is necessary, Brody. He was your friend for years, but he betrayed your friendship."

"Well, gentleman, I guess you have your answer," Brody says to the ADA and Det.

"Ms. Donaldson, I believe your stipulations are reasonable and I think Mr. Weber will agree with them. I will call his attorney on the way back to Pineville and let you know his answer. Thank you for seeing us. We are very sorry this happened to you," ADA Spencer says. Both men shake Madison and Brody's hands and leave.

Brody sits back on the bed next to Madison. "Baby, are you okay?" he asks her.

"I'm fine. It was just hard to relive that night. I'm so thankful you could figure out I was in trouble and save me before, well, you know."

"Well, now it's lunchtime. If you're a good girl and drink your broth, I might have a little reward for you afterward," Brody says with a grin.

"It's not nice to tease a sick person," Madison says, frowning. Brody smirks and leaves the room to tell Jane that Madison is ready for lunch. After he eats and Jane sits at the island to eat her lunch, Brody pockets a small container Joyce left beside his plate.

"Well, did you drink all your broth?" Brody asks Madison as he walks beside her bed. She nods and makes a face as he sits down. "Close your eyes, and don't open them." He removes a spoon and the small container from his pocket when she does. He opens it and says, "Madison, I want you to keep your eyes closed but open your mouth. Can you do that for me?"

"Okay," she replies as she closes her eyes and opens her mouth. Brody places the spoon in her mouth, and she closes it. "Oh, Brody," Madison whispers and opens her eyes. "It's mac and cheese." She gives him a grin that makes his heart want to burst because his simple act of kindness thrilled Madison.

After she finishes the bite, Brody gives her a few more before telling her that's enough and he will sneak her more after dinner. Tears roll down her cheeks. "Brody, thank you so much."

He wipes her tears away with his thumb. "Anything for you, baby," he says tenderly. Brody's phone pings. He takes his phone from his pocket, reads the message, and types out a response. "Well, you have another visitor." At that moment, Bruce walks into the room where he and Brody shake hands. Then Brody leaves the two alone.

Chapter 44

MADISON

Madison is so happy to see Bruce she cries. He comforts her, and they talk. Bruce tells her Brody called him from inside the ambulance on the way to the hospital. Bruce and Perry arrived at the hospital a few minutes later. He also tells her Brody refused to leave her side and made all the arrangements for Madison to be moved to Knoxville and for the nurse.

Bruce shows her he also brought her a bag with her laptop, underwear, two gowns, and some clothes. He tells her Brody sent him a list of things to bring. "Madison, I'm confused about the underwear Brody asked me to get. He was very particular. She laughs and explains the underwear with the days of the week sewn on them. Next, Madison tells Bruce about the Detective and Assistant District Attorney's visit and everything discussed. Bruce informs her he believes she let Ted off too easily.

Brody sticks his head through the door. "Madison, Wyatt is downstairs wanting to see you."

"Well, this is interesting," Madison says, looking at Bruce, who shrugs. She reaches for Bruce's hand. "Yes, let him in," she tells Brody.

When Wyatt walks into the room, Brody says, "I'm not comfortable with him being here. Do you mind if I stay?" Madison shakes her head, and Brody walks to the opposite side of the bed from Bruce. He sits down near the head of her bed, out of Madison's line of sight and gently pats her shoulder for reassurance.

"Wyatt, what do you want? I know you didn't come to check on my health," Madison demands.

Wyatt smirks. "You're right. I didn't come to check on your health. I came to tell you that you got what you deserve by acting like a whore socializing with rich people who are outsiders. You look horrible by the way." Bruce immediately jumps to his feet with clenched fists.

Madison grabs his arm and yanks on it, signaling Bruce to sit back down. "Wyatt, I have had enough of you and all your crap. You have spent most of our lives talking down to me and criticizing me and my decisions," she says. "Now, YOU will listen to what I have to say."

As Wyatt reaches for a chair at the foot of the bed, he says sarcastically, "I'm all ears, Madison."

"No, Wyatt. I don't want you to sit down. I want you to stand like the man you think you are and listen."

Wyatt's face turns a bright shade of red, and he shoves the chair aside. "Okay. If that's what makes you happy."

Madison closes her eyes, takes a deep breath and then asks, "Wyatt, do you remember the night I left you?"

"Of course I do. How could I forget that?"

"Do you remember all of it?"

"Sure and you're wasting my time here reliving the past. What's your point?" Wyatt demands.

Madison takes another deep breath before continuing. "You came home very drunk that night, just like you always did."

"Yeah, so what?"

"I told you that night I was leaving."

"Yeah, you said you couldn't take living on the ranch and that way of life anymore."

"What else did I tell you?" Madison asks. Wyatt looks into Madison's eyes for the first time since he arrived.

"I don't know what you are asking," Wyatt replies, crossing his arms. Madison stares at Wyatt in disbelief, but not surprised.

Bruce squeezes her hand and quietly asks, "Madison, are you sure you want to do this now? Remember, Brody's here too."

She glances at Bruce. "It's time, Bruce because it's long overdue." She turns back to Wyatt and glares at him. "I asked you a question, Wyatt. What else did I tell you that night?"

"I don't remember you telling me anything else. I guess I was too drunk," Wyatt answers, looking confused.

Brody looks at Madison and notices her left-hand clenches into a tight fist. He reaches for it as he looks up at Bruce. Bruce looks back and shakes his head.

"I told you I was pregnant, and the ranch was no place to raise a child so we needed to get away from there. Do you remember that, Wyatt?" Madison asks. Wyatt shakes his head. "Do you remember what happened next, Wyatt?" He looks down at the floor.

Again, Brody looks at Bruce, who is watching Madison. Tears flow from Bruce's eyes. Brody decides it's time for Wyatt to go and quickly stands up.

"Brody, please sit down," Madison demands in an icy voice, and he does. "Okay, Wyatt. Since you don't remember, I'm going to tell you. You got angry. You got so furious that you beat me with your fists and then you stomped and kicked me. You called me every name in the book. By the time you passed out, I was bleeding from every orifice of my body. I crawled across the floor, opened the door, and crawled out onto the porch. Lucky for me, Bruce walked up about that time."

"I heard you screaming at Madison and what sounded like the house being torn apart. Everyone did, but they were too afraid of you to come out and see what was happening," Bruce says. "I saw Madison crawl out of the house. She was bleeding so badly. Back then, we didn't have 911, so I went into the house to get you to call for an ambulance. You were passed out in a chair with Madison's blood all over your clothes, face and hands."

"You're lying," Wyatt yells. "Both of you made up this story to hurt me."

"It's the truth, Wyatt," Bruce says. "Your parents came running to the house because they heard the screaming too. They wouldn't let me call for an ambulance. They told me to take Madison to the hospital. I carried her broken, bloody body to my car and drove her to the hospital as fast as I could." Bruce's tears have turned into full-blown sobs by this time, and he can't continue to speak.

Brody listens as the story unfolds, horrified. He looks from Bruce to Wyatt to Madison. "Wyatt, I was in the hospital for a month. I lost the baby. You beat me so severely that I had to have a hysterectomy. Several of my organs had to be repaired, and two removed. In addition, I had to have plastic surgery to repair one of my eye sockets. This beating I got from Ted is nothing compared to what I got from you."

"I don't believe you. I would have gone to jail if that had really happened," Wyatt says with a smirk.

Madison remains stoic and replies quietly. "No, you didn't go to jail because you were Wyatt Johnson. Your parents owned the sheriff and half the county, so no charges were brought against you. Your parents paid all my medical expenses, which took a year, and they paid for the divorce. Your parents had to agree not to let you leave the ranch alone until I moved away, and they also had to force you to stop drinking."

Wyatt stares at Madison for what seems to be an eternity before saying, "I remember not being able to leave the ranch alone and having to stop drinking. I never knew why though. My parents said you left for good when they gave me the divorce papers to sign."

For the first time, Madison's voice is filled with hate as she says, "thanks to you, Wyatt, I could have no more children. My body is so hideous from all the scars. I don't have sex in the daytime and only in darkness at night. I don't let men see my body because the one time I did, a man got sick in his stomach and threw up all over me. The good thing is I got away from you and that town. I got an education and a career that I loved. But, because of you, I have never loved or trusted another man."

Wyatt looks away from Madison to Bruce, who has laid his head on the bed. Bruce's body quaking from his sobs. Next, he looks at Brody, who has tears running down his cheeks. Then, finally, his eyes return to Madison. "I can see why you hate me so much."

"Wyatt, I don't hate you. I did for many, many years. Now I feel nothing but pity for you," Madison says.

"Pity? Why do you pity me?"

"Because all you ever wanted was a son to carry on your name and leave the ranch to when you die. But, you've only had daughters. Wyatt, the baby I was carrying, was your son. YOUR only son, and you killed him." Madison takes a deep, cleansing breath and says, "Wyatt, I want you to leave now and I never want to see or speak to you again."

Wyatt slowly turns and walks to the doorway. He looks over his shoulder at Madison. "I guess it's too late to say I'm sorry," Wyatt says somberly, leaving.

Madison lays her hand on Bruce's head. "Bruce, it's over now. The truth is out. This has been very hard for you so why don't you go home to Perry and get some rest?"

Bruce raises his head as he wipes his nose and eyes. "What about you, Madison? Are you going to be okay?"

She smiles tenderly at him. "Bruce, it feels good to finally get that off my chest. I'll be fine, and I'll be home bugging you in a few days." Madison runs her fingers across his cheek. "You are my dear brother.

You always have been, and you always will be. I love you with all my heart."

Bruce looks at Madison. "You just told Wyatt that you never loved another man."

"That was after Wyatt. I loved you a long time before that," Madison replies.

"Let's not tell Perry. You know how jealous he can be," Bruce says with a wink and a smile.

"Deal. Now go home to Perry." Bruce rises, kisses Madison's cheek, and leaves the bedroom. Once Madison hears the elevator doors open and close, signaling Bruce is gone, she lies back on the bed and allows herself to cry forgetting Brody is still in the room.

Chapter 45

BRODY

Brody wipes the tears from his face, stands, and walks around to the other side of the bed, listening to Madison's heart-wrenching sobs. Then, finally, Brody does the only thing he knows to do. He carefully gets onto the bed beside her and gently takes her into his arms, trying his best not to hurt her healing body. He holds her tenderly and lets her cry herself to sleep.

Two hours later, Madison's movements wake Brody, and he slowly opens his eyes to see her watching him. "Brody," she whispers.

"I'm right here, baby."

"I'm sorry you had to hear all that. Maybe I should have told you the story before this."

"I knew there had to be a story. Bruce alluded to it the other night but didn't tell me. Instead, he said it was your story to tell when you were ready."

Madison shakes her head. "Some story, huh? The sad tale of Madison Donaldson's life.

"Do you mind explaining Bruce's role other than rescuing you and being your friend?" Brody gently asks.

"Dear, sweet Bruce," Madison sighs. "Bruce and I were in the same class since first grade and have always been friends. I have always known Bruce was gay, and I loved him for not being afraid to be himself. Wyatt and my brother were two years older and teased him constantly. Bruce's parents ignored him, so he spent much time at my house."

"Okay, but I'm still confused."

"Oh, I guess I left out an essential part of the story. Bruce is Wyatt's brother, or he was. Bruce was forced to live and work on the ranch while Wyatt did it by choice. When Bruce took me to the hospital that night, he was so angry and disgusted by his parent's reaction to the beating he never went back. So instead, Bruce lived with my parents and me. He borrowed money from my dad and legally changed his name the next week to distance himself from the Johnson family."

Brody digests the information and then asks, "what happened next?"

"Well, my mom worked, so after I went home from the hospital, Bruce took care of me until mom got home. My brother blamed me for what happened and took Wyatt's side of course. He moved to Seattle after I got home. Once I was well enough, Bruce and I moved to Louisville. We shared an apartment, took out student loans, and went to school. My parents had little money, but they helped us as much as possible. Everyone thought Bruce and I were a couple because we were inseparable. We both worked part-time jobs at a bank. I worked in Human Resources, and Bruce worked in finance. After graduation, the bank hired us full-time and paid for our MBAs. I stayed with the bank and moved up. Bruce quit after a few years and started his financial services business."

"Did you and Bruce still live together?"

"Yes, until I got transferred to Denver. Bruce returned to Pineville and moved his business there. After I left, Bruce finally started exploring his sexuality. A couple of years later, he met and fell in love with Perry. They've been together ever since."

Brody hesitates for a few seconds and then asks, "what about you?"

"What about me?" Madison looks at Brody. "Oh, you mean, did I date?" Brody nods. "No, not for a long time. It took many years for me to trust anyone other than Bruce. Then, finally, I had a boss, older than me and very patient. I trusted him somewhat. He understood my issues with my body. We had a few pleasant months, and then I got transferred to Seattle. I haven't had a long-term relationship with anyone since Wyatt. I met no one I wanted to get that close or trust again."

"Do you ever think you will?"

"Brody, at my age, I think that ship has sailed."

"You're still a young woman, Madison. A man would be lucky to have you as his partner in life."

"That's sweet of you to say." Madison gives Brody a sad smile. "My age and my body aren't something men desire."

"It is if it's the right man," Brody whispers in her ear, making her tingle all over.

"Brody, thank you for holding me and letting me cry."

"Any time, baby," Brody says, kissing her forehead tenderly. "Did Bruce bring the things I asked him to?'

"He said he did. I had to explain about the underwear. That reminds me. I need another Saturday pair of boxers."

"Why is that?"

"Well, Ted tore them off me that night."

Brody is shocked. "You really had them on? I thought you were kidding."

"Nope. I was wearing them. I wonder what Ted thought when he was tearing them off me. He probably thought I was a cross-dresser who couldn't remember what day of the week it was." Madison giggles making Brody laugh out loud. "I love your laugh, Brody. I wish you did it more often," Madison whispers caressing his cheek.

"You make me laugh, baby. Now, I better go see about another pair of Saturday boxers. It will be Saturday a few days."

"Brody, would you hand me my laptop first? I need to check my email since I have clients to tend to. I wonder when I'll get my phone from the police."

"It's here. The Detective texted me he forgot to give it to you. He left it with security downstairs." Brody retrieves her laptop and goes in search of Joyce to get a replacement pair of boxers for Madison and her phone.

Chapter 46

MADISON

Madison is checking her emails when Brody walks back into the suite. "Brody, don't you need to go to work?"

"Nope, I took your advice and let my second in command, Mike, run the office to find out how he does. Angela is monitoring my calls and emails. The calls go to Mike, and most of the emails. She sends me the critical ones. Mike emails or texts whenever he has questions. That way, I can devote almost all my time to caring for you." Brody smiles and climbs onto the bed close to Madison. "Here's your phone."

The pair spends several minutes checking their emails. Then, suddenly, Madison's phone rings. She picks it up and looks at it. "Brody, it says it's Lauren."

"That's weird. Put it on speaker and answer it."

"Hello."

"You bitch. It wasn't enough to take Brody from me, but now you're taking Ted. How dare you lie about him attacking you? Ted wouldn't hurt anyone because he's a kind soul. Brody is not the man you think he is. You'll find out. He's depraved and into all kinds of kinky things. You'll be sorry you ever met him." Then, Lauren hangs up.

Madison looks at Brody. "What was that all about?"

"It sounds like she's drunk or high. There's no telling what Ted told her, and she'll believe every word he says. Ted's always been her go-to guy when no one else wants anything to do with her. But, unfortunately, she's just as depraved as he is. So don't pay any attention to her."

"This day just gets better and better. Thank goodness it's almost bedtime," Madison sighs. She continues checking her emails. "Brody, an email just popped up from Lauren."

"Open it, and let's see what she says," Brody says as he continues checking his emails.

Madison opens the email to find a picture. The room is dimly lit, and the walls are red. Lauren is naked and tied to a Saint Andrews cross against one wall. Various canes, whips, and belts are hanging on the wall beside her. Lauren is smiling into the camera as Brody stands behind her naked. He is holding a whip and appears to be whipping Lauren. His body shows him to be sexually excited.

"Uh, Brody. You better look at this."

He closes his laptop and looks over at Madison's. "Oh, my God! Madison, that's not me. I've done nothing like that in my life," Brody says in horror. "I've never been in a room like that." He stares at the picture. "Wait, I was in a room like that once. Ted had one built and showed it to me." Brody takes the laptop from Madison and types on it.

"What are you doing?" Madison asks.

"I just emailed the picture to myself. We have been working on software to enhance pictures and videos for security. It's far from finished, but I want to try it on this picture." Brody hands Madison back her laptop. As he opens his, she closes hers.

"Can I watch?"

"Sure, baby. I'm going to prove to you that's not me."

"Brody, you don't have to prove it to me. If you tell me it's not you, I believe you. I trust you."

"Madison," Brody reaches for her hand, "thank you for saying that. It means a great deal to me. Now, let's see what the software can do."

She watches as Brody opens the software and loads the picture into it. Then, he manipulates the image in several ways. Madison watches, fascinated, as his fingers fly over the keyboard.

"Okay. Look at this," Brody tells her, pointing at the picture. "The head is not proportional to the body. It's too large. That tells me Lauren or whoever photoshopped the head onto the picture."

"I see it," she says excitedly.

"Now look at this spot on the arm. Can you see it's blurry?" Brody looks at Madison as he points to the spot. She nods. "Something was erased. Now, look at the inside of the calf on the far leg. It's a tattoo of a snake."

"It is. I wonder who the man is," Madison says.

"It's Ted," Brody answers quietly.

"Are you sure?"

"I'm sure. I remember when Ted got the tattoo. He couldn't wait to show it to me and insisted I get one like it." Brody hangs his head.

"Do you have any tattoos?"

"No, baby. I don't. Do you?" She shakes her head. "Well, this software is further along than I thought. That's a good thing. Now, you've had a long day. Are you ready for bed?" he asks, closing his laptop.

"Brody, would you get Jane? I want a shower before bed. I don't know how you've slept beside me without gagging."

"I'd never tell you if I did," he kisses her cheek as he climbs off the bed. "I'll go get Jane for you."

Madison lies her head back on the bed. She believed Brody when he said the man wasn't him, or she wanted to believe him. *I really don't know that much about him. It's good to know positively that it's not* him in the picture. I'm also getting well enough that I need to go to the spare bedroom and let him have his privacy back.

"So I hear somebody wants a shower," Jane says, walking into the bedroom.

"Yes, please. I can't stand myself anymore. Jane, it's almost time for me to move to the spare bedroom, isn't it?"

"Madison, that's your decision. I'm not sure Mr. McGuire will agree. I think he enjoys sleeping next to you. He seems to sleep like a baby."

"I guess from your standpoint, the arrangement is weird."

"Not really. He wants to protect you. I understand that."

"Yeah, but with Ted moving out of state, there's no reason to protect me anymore," Madison adds wistfully.

Jane helps Madison to the shower and then with undressing. Madison insists on bathing herself, so Jane sits on a chair in case Madison needs help. Madison washes her hair and stands under the showerhead enjoying the warm water flowing over her body. She looks down at her bruised body, which is finally healing. Madison is careful when she washes her left side where the broken ribs are. As she washes her chest, abdomen, and stomach, tears flow from her eyes. Now Brody knows about her scars and her fear of anyone seeing them. Her scars would turn him off if they were to start a relationship. Oh well, Brody isn't interested in that kind of relationship, anyway. I need to keep my feelings about him to myself.

Jane helps Madison put on a gown Bruce brought today. Then together, they dry Madison's hair. Finally, Jane helps Madison back into bed and tells Brody they are finished.

"Madison, I just got word that Ted has gone to Florida, so I'll dismiss the security guards except for the one on the ground floor. I still want one to monitor who enters the building," Brody says as he steps into the room. "Also, something significant has come up, and I need go into the office tomorrow. Will you be okay without me for a few hours?"

"I'll be fine, Brody. Jane is here with me. You do whatever you need to do." He climbs onto the bed. "Brody, I can't stay in your room much longer. I'm getting better every day, and you need your privacy. I think I'll move into the spare bedroom in a couple of days."

"Oh," a surprised Brody says. "I like you being in here and sleeping next to me, but if that's how you feel, I can't stop you. You know you're welcome to stay here as long as you like."

"I know, but I need to move home soon. I need to clean the house. I bet it's a mess."

"Bruce and Perry took care of that for you. Will you be comfortable going to the house, or would you rather go to the cabin?"

Madison thinks for a few moments. Then she says, "I think with these broken ribs, I better go to the house. Brody, I appreciate everything you've done for me. I hope you know that."

"That's what friends are for," he says in a hushed tone and reaches over to turn the bedside light off. "Good night, Madison." He turns over away from her.

Madison looks over at him, confused. Did I say something to hurt his feelings? Maybe I need to move sooner than I planned.

Chapter 47

BRODY

Brody is up and gone before Madison wakes. He slept little, thinking about what she said about moving to the spare bedroom and going home. Why does that upset me, he wonders? I'm happy she's getting better, and I knew this time would come, but I enjoy having her in my bed and my apartment.

Angela greets him with a good morning. Brody nods and goes straight to his office. She follows with a cup of coffee.

"Well, I expected you to be more chipper since you haven't been in the office for a week. How's Madison?"

"She's getting better every day. She's talking about going home soon," Brody answers.

"Hmmm. How do you feel about that?"

"I'm glad she's getting better."

"I meant about the going home part. I get the impression that's what is causing this grumpy demeanor."

"I got little sleep, is all. Where's Mike?" Brody asks, cutting Angela off. "I need to find out where we are on the Baltimore deal."

"The deal is ready to go," Mike says, walking into the office. "All that's needed is for you to go, meet the man, and sign the papers."

"Great," Brody says. "Call him and see if we can meet tomorrow."

"Uh, tomorrow's Saturday, Brody," Mike says.

"I know what day tomorrow is. Just call him," Brody says sharply, looking at Mike.

"Yes, sir. I'm on it." Mike turns quickly and leaves the office.

"You didn't have to bite his head off," Angela states. "Now, what do I need to do and please tell me in a civilized voice?"

"I need a meeting with my lawyer and accountant now." Angela nods and leaves the office. Brody takes a sip of coffee and looks out the window. Angela was right. He's angry about Madison leaving, but why? Why is that bothering me so much?

Brody's intercom buzzes, interrupting his thoughts. He rereads the email he received from Ted's attorney late last night. The offer to sell Ted's law firm to Brody is Ted's way of apologizing. What a damn mess, Brody thinks.

"Mr. McGuire, your attorney, and accountant are on their way up. I'll bring coffee." Two minutes later, Angela steps in with a pot of coffee and cups, which she sits down on the credenza. As she leaves, the attorney and accountant walk in.

"Gentlemen, please sit down. I have something that is time sensitive to discuss. For reasons I can't talk about, Ted Weber has moved to Florida and wants to sell me his business. He has offered to sell it at fifty cents on the dollar. That's a great price, but I am not interested in his law firm. Suggestions, please, gentlemen."

"Do you think that's his last offer, or would he come down lower?" the accountant asks.

"He's in legal trouble, so he might come down a little, but not much," Brody answers. "Excuse me," he says as his intercom buzzes. "Yes, Angela?"

"Mike says tomorrow at 1:00 pm is acceptable. When would you like to leave?" Angela asks.

"Have the jet ready at 8:00 am, please. Thanks, Angela."

"Now, gentlemen, back to our topic at hand," Brody says.

"I think you could make a good profit. I don't think you would have any trouble selling the company," the attorney says. "In fact, I know two or three men that would definitely be interested. So even if you bought it at half the value, you could easily sell it at a twenty-five percent markup."

"How would we find out what the company is worth?"

The attorney ponders the question for several seconds. "I would have to look at their client list. I know they handle a few big-name companies. Why you, Brody?"

"Let's just say Ted owes me. How long will it take to evaluate the company? I want this over with as soon as possible."

"I can start on it today," the attorney answers.

"And I can look at their financials this afternoon. All we need is for Mr. Weber to talk to his people about releasing the information to us."

"Great," Brody says. "I'll let you know as soon as that's done." After the gentlemen leave, Brody emails Ted's attorney concerning access to the company's financials and the client list. In fifteen minutes, he has the names of people who need to be contacted. Brody sends the information to his attorney and accountant immediately.

Next, Brody texts Joyce and tells her he needs a bag packed for a meeting and an overnight stay tomorrow with a client out of state. He tells her he won't be back until Sunday afternoon.

Then, Brody gets on the phone with the developer for the software program he used on the picture last night. Without going into details about the picture, Brody describes what he did and makes several suggestions for product improvement.

By the time he hangs up on the call, it is 4:00. He walks out to Angela's desk to pick up everything he needs for the meeting and contract signing tomorrow. "I'll see you on Monday," he tells Angela, walking out the door.

"I hope you'll be in a better mood by then," she yells after him.

"Don't bet on it," Brody yells back from the elevator. He gets into his pickup but doesn't drive to the apartment. Instead, Brody drives toward Pineville, stopping at a lake halfway. He still has his fishing equipment in the back of the pickup, so he grabs it and walks down to the lake. However, Brody doesn't fish. Instead, he sits on a rock looking out over the water, contemplating his thoughts and feelings.

After a while, it dawns on Brody that Madison's leaving bothers him so much because it feels like the relationship is ending. He knows she doesn't blame him for what happened with Ted, but there's something else. Something Brody can't put his finger on. Maybe he can get her to talk to him tonight.

Chapter 48

MADISON

Madison is relieved to find Brody gone when she wakes up. I can't think when he's around. I'm tired of lying in this bed beside him, having improper thoughts about a friend. Every waking moment, Madison lies in that bed, wishing Brody would kiss her on the lips instead of on the forehead or cheek. His warm body next to her drives her wild with desire. Well, today's the day to move, she decides.

"Good morning, Madison," Jane says, entering the bedroom.

"Jane, I'm moving to the spare bedroom today."

"Are you sure you're up to climbing the stairs?"

"I have to. I have to get out of Brody's bed and his room. He needs his privacy."

"Madison, I don't think having you here bothered him. I told you he said he enjoys sleeping next to you because he sleeps so well."

"Jane, I have to move, and I need to go home. Soon." Madison struggles to sit up on the side of the bed. Jane reaches to help, but Madison shakes her head. Then, finally, she makes it and stares at her lap.

Jane sits on the side of the bed and takes Madison's hand. "Madison, there's more to it. As a woman, I can tell you're struggling with something." Jane studies Madison and then says "you've fallen in love with him, haven't you?"

Tears flow down Madison's cheeks. "Yes," she mutters.

"It's okay, Madison. He's a wonderful man."

"No, it's not okay, Jane. We are supposed to be friends, and that's all. I'm not supposed to feel this way about him. Besides, I'm older than him, and he doesn't feel the same way."

Jane squeezes her hand. "Have you talked to Brody about this?"

"Oh no. That would definitely end our friendship. I enjoy spending time with Brody and we have fun together," Madison says.

"I think you should be honest with him. If it ends the friendship, maybe there wasn't a genuine friendship there after all."

"I can't. I just can't."

"Okay. Believe me, I understand, but just think about it. You have all day before Brody returns home. Now, if you're serious about moving, let's get up try those stairs."

Madison and Jane leave the bedroom and head for the stairs. While Jane stays at the foot of the stairs, Madison slowly climbs up. When she reaches the landing, Madison turns and waves to Jane.

Movement in the kitchen catches Madison's eyes. "Look, Joyce. I can climb the stairs, so I'll be moving today."

Joyce walks to the bottom of the stairs and stands next to Jane. "Madison, are you sure? Mr. McGuire will not be pleased."

"It's okay," Madison replies. "I told him last night that I was much better and would be moving." She sees Joyce give Jane a questioning look. Jane shrugs her shoulders and walks off.

Madison spends the day walking around the apartment and going up and down the stairs. She tires easily but refuses to let Jane see. Madison takes a nap in the upstairs bedroom after lunch and dreams of Brody making love to her. She wakes with a smile on her face, but when she realizes it was only a dream, she cries silently.

Brody was expected to return for dinner, but he never shows. A disappointed Madison sits at the dining room table and eats alone. After dinner, she returns to the guest bedroom and checks her emails. She finds one from her friend in Baltimore, telling Madison he no longer needs her services. He has a buyer for his company.

Madison goes downstairs in search of Joyce. She finds her in Brody's bedroom, packing a bag for him. "Joyce, when will Brody be home?"

"I'm not sure. Brody messaged me earlier to pack a bag for him, saying he had to go out of town early in the morning and will be back on Sunday. Can I help you with anything?"

"No, I was just wondering. I think I'll wait for him in the library. Thanks."

Madison sits in a chair facing the door and waits for Brody. She contemplates precisely what to say to him. Jane said she should tell Brody the truth. But if I do, not only will I lose our friendship, I'll lose him. Do I really want that?

Chapter 49

BRODY

I t's 9:00 when Brody arrives home. He walks into his bedroom and tosses his suit jacket and tie on a chair. He turns, expecting to see Madison in his bed, but the bed is empty and freshly made. On it sits his packed bag for tomorrow."

"Madison! Madison, where are you?" Brody calls, walking into the kitchen.

"I'm in the library."

He finds Madison sitting in a chair facing the doorway. "Hey, you're up and out of bed. That's great. How do you feel?" Brody asks trying to sound happy.

"I'm good, Brody. You're home late."

"I know. I had some things to take care of at the office." Madison nods. "I see you moved out of the bedroom. I wasn't expecting it this soon."

"I feel good, so I decided it was time for me to leave you alone."

"You didn't have to, you know. I told you I enjoyed you being there," Brody says, watching Madison. He walks over and sits in a chair across from her.

"Brody, I got an email from my friend in Baltimore today. He said he no longer needed my services. Joyce said you are going out of town in the morning. Is there a correlation between those two events?" Madison suggests, looking directly into Brody's eyes.

"Yes, Madison. I'm buying his company."

"Why, Brody?"

"Do you want the standard business answers or my personal answer?"

Madison studies his face and then replies, "the personal one, please."

"The personal answer is that I hate to see anyone lose their job and insurance. By purchasing the company, I can ensure I save jobs. Also, by bringing his employees into my company, I can provide better medical benefits and higher salaries. Plus, your friend remains with the company and can go back to doing what he loves most: developing games."

"That's a good reason."

"Do you doubt me?"

"No, Brody. You're a decent man. I trust your judgment and thank you for caring about my friend and his people."

"You're welcome, Madison, and yes, that's why I'm going to Baltimore tomorrow. Mike handled all the details and negotiations and did a wonderful job. I still have to meet your friend and sign the contract. The sooner, the better for him and his employees."

"Okay, Brody." Madison stands. "I need to go home. I won't be here when you come back." She walks out of the room.

Brody stares after her. *I won't be here when you get back* runs through his mind repeatedly like a broken record. *Is she upset because I bought the company?* Brody runs up the stairs, throws open the door, and finds Madison sitting on the bed, staring at her hands lying in her lap.

"Are you upset that I bought the company? Is that why you're leaving so soon?" he demands.

"No, no, Brody. It's not that," Madison answers, not looking at him.

Brody walks over to her and kneels in front of her. "Madison, tell me why you're leaving. I deserve to know the truth." He lifts her chin to find tears in her eyes.

"Yes, I guess you do." Madison draws a deep breath and the tears run down her cheeks. "Brody, I have more feelings toward you than I ever expected."

Brody looks at her. "I'm confused. Please explain?"

"Every night, I've lain in bed next to you, wishing you would kiss and make love to me. I know I shouldn't have those feelings. We're friends, but I can't help how I feel. It's just an older woman's fantasy of us being more than friends. I need to get my head wrapped around these feelings and return to a friendship mind frame. I need distance from you, Brody."

Brody looks deep into her eyes. "Are, are you saying you love me?" Madison nods and wipes the tears away. "I don't know what to say." Brody stands. "This isn't at all what we agreed to." He turns and walks out of the room.

He walks into his room and slams the door hard. Oh, wow! Madison's fallen in love with me. What do I do now? This isn't what I want. I want someone to spend time with and have fun with. But I don't want to be in a relationship with this woman. She's older than I am. She wants to out some distance between us so she can think. Well, that's a good thing. It will give me time to decide how to end this relationship.

Brody undresses and climbs into bed, knowing he must get up early. He realizes he misses Madison's body next to his, but it is time for her to go. Sleep comes much later, and when it does, it brings memories of Madison. Memories of holding her in his arms as they danced and touching her silky skin. Gently kissing her beautiful lips as she slept next to him. Running his fingers through her silver hair and memorizing her womanly scent of lavender and vanilla.

Finally, the alarm goes off. The sheets are wet with sweat. Brody's body is on fire with a need for release. He finds that release in the shower, and it drains what little energy he has left. Brody forces himself to shave and dress. He then leaves the apartment before anyone wakes, including Joyce.

Chapter 50

BRODY

The apartment is too quiet when Brody returns home on Sunday night. His plane landed at 4:00, but he deliberately stayed away until 10:00, knowing Madison wouldn't be there. So instead, he sat at a bar with his dear and only close friend, named bourbon.

Brody's not drunk, well, not yet, but soon. He walks through every room, wishing to find Madison, but he knows he won't. In fact, there's no evidence anywhere that she was ever there. Only Brody's memories of her voice, her giggle, and her scent. Her scent! He goes into the ensuite of Madison's bedroom. There it is—the familiar lavender and vanilla. Brody leans against the counter for several minutes, inhaling the scent and contemplating what it would be like to shower with Madison and wash her with her favorite body wash.

Finally, he shakes his head and returns to the kitchen, where he grabs a bottle of bourbon and goes to the only room Madison spent hardly any time in—his game/poker room. Brody opens the bottle and lies down on the leather sofa. That's where he remains, only leaving to get more bourbon.

Wednesday morning, Brody wakes up needing to know how Madison is. He remembers she has a doctor's appointment at 1:00 pm. He doesn't bathe or shave. Instead, he borrows sunglasses, a baseball cap, and binoculars from George. Brody drives to a car rental company renting a plain white car that will blend nicely with Madison's neighborhood.

Brody makes a plan on the drive to Pineville. Once there, he puts his plan into action. Brody parks the car across the street two doors down from Madison's house. From this viewpoint, he can watch her front door. Pulling the baseball cap low on his head, Brody puts on the sunglasses, slumps down in the seat, and waits.

At 12:30, a car pulls into Madison's driveway. Brody picks up the binoculars and watches as Perry gets out and goes inside Madison's house. Minutes later, he comes out and opens the car's passenger door. After a few seconds, Madison steps out of the house, turns and locks the door, and slowly begins walking toward the car. Brody looks closely at her and feels the air sucked from his lungs. Madison is pale with dark circles under her eyes. She is thinner than she was the last time he saw her. Brody watches as she gets into Perry's car. He waits until the vehicle is down the street before he leaves and returns home. At least I know Bruce and Perry are looking out for her, but he determines quickly that doesn't make me feel better.

Once home with another bottle of bourbon, Brody goes back into the game/poker room, where he remains the rest of the day, and into the night, thankful he doesn't dream or think if he drinks enough.

Chapter 51

BRODY

"Well, it's about time you showed up at the company you own," Angela states Thursday morning when Brody steps off the elevator.

"Angela, you're fired," Brody says, walking to his door, not looking her way.

"Is that before or after your cup of coffee?"

"After. Definitely after," Brody replies.

Minutes later, Angela walks in with his coffee and sits it on the desk. "For someone that bought a fantastic company over the weekend that will increase his diversity and profit margin, you are a sad sack. What happened?" She plops in his chair, leaving him to stand or sit across from the desk.

Brody stares at her and then sits down. "Madison went home."

"That's great news. I'm glad she's better." Angela pauses, studying Brody. "But that's not what has you so upset, is it?"

"You know me too well. I need an assistant that doesn't know me or anything about me."

"Brody, look at me," Angela demands, and he does slowly. She sees nothing but pain in his eyes. "What's going on?"

"Before she left, she told me she had fallen in love with me."

"Is that a bad thing, Brody?"

"Of course, it is. We agreed to be friends only. I don't want that type of relationship with her or anyone else."

Angela watches Brody as he slumps farther down in the chair. "Did she say anything else?"

"Yeah, she said she needed to put some distance between us and get her thoughts together or some crap like that. I don't remember her exact words."

"What are you going to do about it?"

Brody laughs. "What am I going to do? Nothing. Absolutely nothing. She wants distance. She gets distance. So I won't bother her."

"So you lost a good friend and returned to your old friend, Mr. Bourbon. You are such an idiot, Brody. Are you furious because one, you lost a friend? Two,
because Madison is in love with you? Or three, because you didn't have the guts
to express that you're in love with her?" Angela stands and stomps out of the office.

"What did you just say?" Brody yells at Angela.

"You heard me," she yells back.

Brody rises and goes to sit in his chair. Angela's words replay in his mind. Are you angry because you lost Madison as a friend? Because Madison has fallen in love with you? Or because you didn't tell her you're in love with her? What kind of crazy pills is Angela taking? I'm in love with Madison. Of course not. That's preposterous.

His intercom buzzes. "Brody, Nancy from HR needs to see you immediately."

"Send her in."

"Mr. McGuire," Nancy says, walking in. "We have an urgent HR-related matter, and I honestly do not know how to handle it. It involves one of our best employees."

"Please sit down, Nancy." Brody presses the intercom button. "Angela, grab Mike, and you both come in here."

Angela and Mike arrive in the office quickly and sit down. Nancy explains the urgent matter.

"I agree this needs to be handled carefully and quickly," Brody says. "Here's what I want you to do. Angela, take notes, please. Nancy, call Madison Donaldson and ask for her help. Do not under any circumstances mention my name. You can call me the boss, owner, or whatever, but not my name. If Ms. Donaldson has questions, she can deal with Mike. You can tell Ms. Donaldson that she came highly recommended." Brody stops and thinks for a few seconds before continuing.

"Next, if Ms. Donaldson agrees to help, I will give her free rein to all records. She can decide how best to handle the situation, and money is unimportant."

"By money, you mean her consultation costs?" Mike asks.

Brody looks at the three people. "That and if she determines we need a new HR program, plan, or procedures. Ms. Donaldson is free to spend money however she sees fit. I trust her judgment fully, and I doubt she will spend money unwisely. Questions?" Everyone shakes their head. "Good. Nancy, make the call now and let me know as soon as you have her answer. Angela, if she agrees, make a room reservation for Ms. Donaldson at the best hotel in the city. Thank you, everyone."

Everyone leaves except Angela. She closes the door and turns to Brody. "Why not use your name?"

"Because she doesn't know I own BM Technologies. If she knew, she probably wouldn't take the job. Nancy really needs her help, and so does the company." Angela nods.

Chapter 52

MADISON

Madison sits at her dining table, staring at her kitchen. *I should eat something, but I don't have an appetite. I can't remember the last time I ate. Oh, yes, I do. It was Friday night. The night I told Brody I had feelings for him. The night I ended our friend-ship.*

She reaches for the phone next to her as it rings, hoping it's Brody. Unfortunately, she hasn't heard a word from him. But it's not, so she answers it.

"Hello."

"Ms. Donaldson?"

"Yes, this is she."

"Ms. Donaldson, my name is Nancy Harris. I'm the director of HR for BM Technologies in Knoxville."

"What can I do for you?" Madison says.

"We have a complicated issue with one of our best and brightest employees. The situation needs to be resolved quickly and quietly so I would like your help. I've never had an issue like this before."

Madison is quiet and then asks, "why me?"

"My boss said you came highly recommended, and personally, Ms. Donaldson, I've been a fan of yours all my career. My boss said you are to have access to anything you need, and money is no object. That means your fees, your solution to the problem, and any recommendations you have to prevent this from happening again. Also, you are to have the final say on the future of this employee."

"Wow," Madison says. "This must be a serious issue."

"It is and a valuable employee we would rather not lose, if possible," Nancy adds.

"Well, it just so happens I'm currently available. I'll be happy to help. Is Monday morning a good time to meet and begin work on this problem?"

"Monday is perfect. I'll email you the address and my contact information. Thank you so much, Ms. Donaldson. I look forward to working with you."

When Madison ends the call, she looks toward the kitchen again. "Well, at least I have something to look forward to and hopefully keep my mind occupied for a few days," she says aloud. "I guess I better eat something so my clothes don't fall off me."

Chapter 53

BRODY

Brody ponders the issue Nancy brought to his attention when she calls him.

"Mr. McGuire, Ms. Donaldson has agreed to help. She will be here first thing Monday morning."

"That's great news, Nancy. I hope between the two of you; this issue can be resolved quickly. Please let Angela know to make the room reservation."

"I don't want to be here while Madison is here. Where can I go?" Brody says aloud. "Oh yeah. I bought that deep sea fishing expedition at the auction." He pulls the receipt from the auction out of his desk and finds the website. Next, he calls the company and makes a reservation that begins Friday morning and ends the following Thursday night. That will work out perfectly with my schedule. I have to be back that Friday night for the wrap-up meeting of the zoo gala. He stands up, puts his jacket on, and walks to Angela's desk.

"Angela, I need the jet to fly me to Key West, Florida, tomorrow and pick me up a week from Friday. I also need hotel reservations and a rental car. I won't be in tomorrow. I will be back in time to attend the wrap-up meeting for the board of the zoo gala. When you get the information, please send it to me." Brody turns and walks to the elevator.

"So you plan to be gone while Madison is here?" Angela asks. Brody nods. "Chicken," she yells at him.

"You're fired," Brody yells.

"Thanks. I'll see you when you get back." Brody waves and steps onto the elevator.

Chapter 54

MADISON

Nancy emailed Madison all the information, including a hotel reservation, so Madison drives to Knoxville Sunday night. She is too excited about the job to sleep much and is up and at BM Technologies at 8:00 am. Her first order of business is to meet the owner, who has given Madison Carte Blanc over everything related to the HR issue.

Madison rides the elevator to the top floor of the high rise and steps off into a beautifully decorated reception area. The desk is empty, so Madison looks down a hallway to her right and sees no one. She turns to her left and is shocked to see a portrait of Brody hanging on the wall. She approaches the painting, and her heart beats faster.

Brody is in a dark gray suit with a light gray shirt and navy tie. His hair is black, so Madison determines the portrait is a few years old. Brody is wearing a big smile making his dark blue eyes crinkle at the corners. She reaches up and runs a finger over the clean-shaven jaw. "Oh, Brody, how I miss you," Madison mutters.

"He's a very handsome man, isn't he?" a voice says behind Madison making her jump. "Sorry, I didn't mean to scare you."

Madison turns around. "Yes, he's very handsome. So Brody, I mean Mr. McGuire, the owner of BM Technologies?"

"Yes, he is. I'm Angela, his assistant. We talked on the phone once when I reserved your cabin for him." Angela offers her hand to Madison.

Madison shakes Angela's hand and says, "yes, I remember you." Madison hesitates for a few seconds. "Angela, I can't do this. I'm sorry." She releases Angela's hand and walks toward the elevator.

"He said you would say that."

Madison stops and turns back. "What?"

"Brody said you wouldn't want the job after you found out he owns the company. But he also said this was professional, not personal, so please stay and help Nancy," Angela says.

"May I speak to Mr. McGuire?"

"I'm afraid he's out of the office until next week."

Madison shakes her head and mutters, "he can't even stay and face me after offering me a job."

Angela over hears Madison's words and says, "Madison, he's confused. Give him some time."

"Angela, I feel you know what's going on, so let me tell you I'm older than Brody. I don't have a lot of time to sit around and wait. Now, where can I find Nancy?"

Chapter 55

MADISON

It takes Madison all week to resolve the employee issue. She has worked long hours and is tired, so Madison is happy today is Friday. She went home after work yesterday to do laundry and pack fresh clothes. Madison leaves tonight on a flight to Spain for a conference and to visit friends. Ben has been texting her all week about his company's HR problem and wants to hire her.

After a quick meeting with Nancy on the second floor, Madison pushes the elevator button to go upstairs for a wrap-up meeting with Mike. Her phone pings with a message. It's Ben again asking her to dinner to discuss the issue. Madison is typing a response when the elevator door opens, and she steps in without looking up from her phone.

"Ms. Donaldson."

Madison looks up into the dark blue eyes of the man she's fallen in love with. "Mr. McGuire," she responds. Madison looks down quickly and resumes typing her response to Ben, but her body is on fire, and her heart beats faster. The elevator rises quickly. When the door opens, Brody extends his hand for Madison to exit first.

Angela looks up. "Madison, Mike is ready for you. Brody, what are you doing here? You said you wouldn't be back until Monday."

Madison quickly walks off, not wanting to hear Brody's response, but she can feel him watching her. The meeting with Mike lasts an hour. He's pleased, which makes Madison happy. She walks toward the elevator smiling.

"Madison," Angela says. "Brody would like a word with you before you leave."

Madison rolls her eyes. "Is he free?"

"Yes. He should be. I stepped away for a couple of minutes, but I'm fairly certain no one is in there. Go on in."

Madison opens the door and finds a smiling Lauren sitting on the corner of Brody's desk. The neckline of Lauren's blouse is so low, and her skirt is so short both almost meet in the middle. Madison hears a sound and turns to her right. Brody walks out of his private bathroom, tucking his shirt into his pants. He looks up and sees Madison just as she turns and runs from the room. She hears him call her name, but she ignores him.

As Madison walks by Angela's desk, she says, "Angela, I don't think he's confused any longer." Then, Madison practically runs to the elevator, which fortunately opens as soon as she punches the button.

Chapter 56

BRODY

"Madison," Brody yells, but she doesn't stop. "Dammit!" He races toward the door, but Lauren steps in his way.

"Let her go, Brody. "We're not through talking."

"Get out of my way Lauren," Brody yells, trying to get around her, but Lauren is persistent and grabs his arm. He shoves her hard, and she falls on the floor. Brody ignores her and walks out of the office.

"She's gone," Angela says sadly.

"Dammit. Lauren, get your ass up and get out of my office, and never set foot in here again," Brody says.

"Fine, but I'll see you tonight at the meeting. You can't avoid me," Lauren says, picking herself up off the floor seductively and walking toward the elevator.

Once she's gone, Angela looks at a sad man. "What now?" she asks.

"I don't know. I really don't know," Brody answers in a pitiful voice, returning to his office, and slamming the door where he remains in isolation until time to leave for the meeting.

As unhappy as he is about Madison leaving his office the way she did, Brody is relieved tonight's meeting has finally come. This wrap-up meeting about the zoo gala is his last duty as a board director. So he breathes a sigh of relief as he walks into the most exclusive restaurant in Knoxville. The hostess recognizes Brody and points him toward a table in the back while he orders a drink from a server who walks past.

Brody looks around the restaurant while waiting for his drink to arrive. He spots Lauren walking toward Ben and a woman that has her back to him. Brody's breath leaves his body as he recognizes the silver shoulder-length hair. His drink arrives quickly, and Brody makes his way toward the table. He overhears the conversation as he walks.

"Lauren," Ben says. "I thought you were in Florida with Ted."

"I was, but I had to return for the final zoo gala meeting. I was the chair of the planning committee," Lauren answers proudly.

"Lauren, do you know Madison?" Lauren looks at Madison with a smirk and nods.

"Hello, Lauren," Madison says. "Florida is so beautiful. I bet your photographic talents are being put to good use capturing all the memories you and Ted are making."

At the same time that Lauren says bitch and walks off; Brody spits his drink all over the back of Madison.

"What the heck?" Madison says.

"I think Brody just spit bourbon all over you," Ben replies jumping up to grab napkins off the table behind him.

"Madison, I'm so sorry," Brody says, grabbing napkins from another table. Ben hands his napkins to Madison while Brody blots her hair and shoulders with his. Finally, he leans over and whispers in her ear. "I couldn't help it. Your comment to Lauren was perfect."

"It was, wasn't it?" Madison says with a giggle only Brody can hear.

"There, I think you're okay for now," Brody says. Then he looks at Ben and feels jealousy overtake him. "What are the two of you doing here?"

"I'm trying to convince Madison to work on a project for me," Ben answers with an evil grin.

"An HR project," Madison quickly adds.

"Well, I'll let you get back to your conversation. It's great to see you both again," Brody says, brushing Madison's arm as he leaves. He is the last one to arrive at his table, and the only chair available has its back to Madison. Brody sits down and glances over his shoulder at her. She is laughing at something Ben said so he turns around. I hope this meeting doesn't last long, he thinks. I can't keep turning my head around to look at Madison.

Unfortunately, the meeting lasts two hours, so when Brody finally stands and looks around, Ben and Madison are gone. Disappointed, Brody says his goodbyes and gets in his car. He grabs his phone and sends a message to Madison.

"Are you still with Ben?"

"No," she answers immediately.

"We need to talk. Where are you staying? I'll come there."

"Yes, we need to talk. I'm not staying anywhere."

"Surely you aren't driving home this late," Brody replies.

"Are you concerned for my safety?"

Brody shakes his head and replies, "Always."

"LOL. I'm on a plane awaiting takeoff."

"Where to?"

"Madrid, if it's any of your business."

"Business or pleasure?"

"Both," Madison replies.

"When are you coming back?"

"Nosy, aren't you?"

"Well?"

"I don't know. I haven't booked a return flight."

"Let me know when you get back," Brody writes, but no response comes. That woman drives me crazy. At least she's not in a hotel room with Ben. That would kill me. Did I just think that? Why would it kill me? Because you are in love with her, you idiot.

202

Chapter 57

BRODY

Two weeks go by and Brody still hasn't heard from Madison. It's driving him crazy. The only thing keeping him sane is purchasing Ted's business and trying to find a buyer simultaneously. Plus, Ted is in prison in Florida, making any contact harder for Ted's attorney to complete the deal.

Finally, Brody gets a message from Madison on Friday afternoon, exactly two weeks after he last saw her.

"Landing in two hours," she says.

"Come to the apartment so we can talk," Brody replies.

"I'm tired. I want a nap."

"You can take a nap at the apartment. I won't bother you."

"I'd rather meet on neutral ground," Madison replies.

"NO," Brody says.

"You're not my boss. Get over yourself."

Madison's reply makes Brody laugh.

"Technically, I haven't signed your check yet because I'm still waiting on an invoice, so yes, I'm still your boss."

Madison's answer is, "rolling my eyes."

"Well?"

"FINE! Your apartment."

Brody smiles because he won the argument. He sends several emails and walks out of his office.

"Well, I believe that's the first time I've seen you smile in over a month," Angela says.

"I'm going home to resolve this problem once and for all. Wish me luck," Brody says, walking toward the elevator. "And I've decided not to fire you until Monday."

"Great," Angela says. "I dreaded spending the weekend looking through the classifieds for a new job."

Once home, Brody changes into a T-shirt and pajama pants. He makes a drink and sits down to wait for Madison. An hour later, the elevator doors open, and there she stands. Brody's breath catches as he looks at the beautiful woman from head to toe. He's missed her so much.

"Hello, Brody," Madison says tentatively.

"Hi, beautiful."

Madison rolls her eyes and walks into the living room slowly. "I want to take a shower first. Then, we can talk and get this over with."

"Okay, if that's what you want," Brody replies. Then, he watches as Madison climbs the stairs. Once she is inside her room, Brody goes to his bedroom and gets a T-shirt. Next, he takes it to her bedroom, sits on the bed, and waits for her.

Madison emerges from the bathroom about twenty minutes later, wearing only a towel. "Well, you must really be in a hurry to have this talk. You couldn't even wait for me to dress."

Brody holds up the T-shirt. "I brought a peace offering," he says with a grin. Madison reaches for it, but he pulls it away. "Talk first."

"Okay, Brody. I'll go first." Madison takes a deep breath and looks straight into Brody's dark blue eyes. "I want to apologize for dumping my feelings on you. I know I caught you off guard, so I didn't expect you to say anything. I'm sorry I let my feelings ruin our friendship because I valued our time together. But I won't apologize for my feelings. You are closer to my ideal man than anyone else I have ever met. I just wish I was younger, or you were older."

Brody stands and walks over to her. He stands so close Madison he can feel her breath on his face. "First, what you saw in my office wasn't what you think. Lauren was angry with me and poured coffee in my lap so I had to change clothes. Second, Madison, I'm the one that owes you an apology. I'm sorry for how I acted when you told me about your feelings. I should have been more sensitive, but I felt confused. I had so many unfamiliar feelings and emotions that I didn't know what to do. When you said you wanted distance between us, that was hard for me, but it gave me time to think and sort things out in the long run."

"Okay, what do you suggest we do now?" Madison says.

Brody can hear the sadness in her voice. "Well, I suggest the first thing I should do is kiss you."

"What?"

"Shut up and kiss me," Brody says, taking her into his arms. One hand goes around her neck and the other on her lower back. He looks into her surprised eyes and leans in to kiss her. The kiss is gentle at first but quickly becomes more demanding. Brody's tongue teases Madison's lips requesting entrance to her mouth.

Madison quickly begins returning Brody's kiss, and when her lips part, Brody's body goes wild. He is burning with desire for this woman. Every inch of his body reacts to her, and he grips her tightly, ensuring she feels it.

After several minutes of feverish kissing, Brody whispers in Madison's ear. "I want to make love to you, baby."

Madison pulls away. "No, Brody. There's too much light in here."

"Even with me, you're concerned about how your body looks?" Madison nods, looking down at the floor. Brody lifts her chin, forcing her to look up at him. "Baby, I've seen your body, and I think it's beautiful."

"You have? When?"

"That night Ted attacked you. He had ripped all your clothes off. When the police pulled him off you, I covered your nakedness with your throw on the sofa."

"And you still want to make love to me in the light?" Madison asks in disbelief.

"Scars help make us who we are. I think of them as a mark of survival." Brody takes two steps back, reaches for the hem of his T-shirt, and pulls it over his head. "Have you ever wondered why you've never seen me without a shirt?" Madison nods, and Brody turns his back to her.

He hears her gasp. "Brody, what happened to your back?"

"Do you remember I said my father took his anger out on us?"

"Yes," Madison whispers."

"To make a long story short, he did this to me the morning he died. He whipped me with a belt and left me on the floor, bleeding, while he sat in a chair, drinking his whiskey and watching TV. My mother came home and kicked him out of the house. He took the only car we had and went to his favorite bar. The police said he left the bar and drove the car into a tree. The car burst into flames, and he died in the fire."

"Oh, Brody," Madison whispers as she places her hands on his shoulders. "Can I touch your back?"

"No one has seen my back except my mother, doctors, and now you. Yes, please touch me, Madison." Brody feels Madison softly run her hands over the scars that run across his entire back. Then she surprises him by tenderly kissing each scar, her warm breath racing toward his groin.

"Brody."

"Yes, baby?"

"Turn around, please."

Brody turns around. As he watches, Madison removes the towel and lets it fall around her ankles. Tears fill his eyes. "Madison, look at me," he says. "I love you with everything I am. You've made me a better person because of your love. I want to earn your trust and love for the rest of my life."

Brody kneels in front of her. His lips softly trace the scar running from Madison's sternum past her belly button to her groin. Then he moves to her scar that runs hip to hip.

"Make love to me, Brody," Madison says, breathlessly. He rises, picks her up, and carries her downstairs, laying her in the center of his bed.

Much, much later, an exhausted Brody and Madison lie in each other's arms.

"Brody, has Mike performed well enough that you can turn most of your business over to him?"

"Yes. Why?"

"Then move in with me. We'll move to the cabin and spend the rest of our lives making love and fishing."

"I like that idea very much. Is tomorrow too soon?"

About Author

Gaylene Nunn is a widowed 60+ year old woman who spent her career in banking, financial services, municipal government, and most recently as CFO for a upper level regional university that she helped create. She retired in 2017 with the title of Vice President Emeritus. Gaylene is a Texas native who enjoys reading, writing, traveling, and spending time with her dog, Sam, and cat, Emily.

Also By

GAYLENE NUNN

"A Second Chance at Love"
"Before Your Loved One Goes—Planning for Your Reality"
"An Eternity of Love"*
"Damaged by Love"*
*Co-authored with Deserie LaCrosse